Gimme Back My Brain

SPINETINGLERS

#23

Gimme Back My Brain

M. T. COFFIN

AN AVON CAMELOT BOOK

This is a work of fiction. Names, characters, places, and incidents either are the product of the author's imagination or are used fictitiously. Any resemblance to actual events, locales, organizations, or persons, living or dead, is entirely coincidental and beyond the intent of either the author or the publisher.

AVON BOOKS
A division of
The Hearst Corporation
1350 Avenue of the Americas
New York, New York 10019

First Avon Camelot Printing: July 1997

CAMELOT TRADEMARK REG. U.S. PAT. OFF. AND IN OTHER COUNTRIES, MARCA REGISTRADA, HECHO EN U.S.A.

Printed in the U.S.A.

OPM 10 9 8 7 6 5 4 3 2 1

For Mary Wollstonecraft Shelley and D. F. Jones, who,
I think, got it right the first time . . .

I

MY NAME IS MAX . . .

Which makes me Max Helvey, idea guy. Ideas are a good thing, and that's how I think about the world, how I divide events up in my mind—into big piles of good things and bad things. I'm thirteen years old, and over the last three years I've lost or broken eight pairs of glasses. Bad thing. If I have to report another loss to my parents, they're going to bolt the next pair to the side of my head, which would be a really bad thing. That's what made looking at this robot interesting: he reminded me of myself, because he had glasses bolted to the side of his head—thick, round frames which made his artificial eyes seem four inches around.

How it was I was looking at a real-life robot I'll get to in a minute. The thing to know now is what he looked like, and the answer to that is one word: *bizarre*. I'd seen hundreds of robots on TV shows and movies, and none of them had ever looked like this; not exactly, anyway.

1

Six feet long—he was lying on a slab, still and silent; the robot would obviously have been taller than I was, if he'd stood up—and his skin was the silver color of aluminum foil from head to foot. He was shaped pretty much like a person. Aside from the fake glasses on his head, there were shifts and folds in his metal skin to suggest that he was wearing a jumpsuit, although the truth was, he wasn't wearing anything at all.

The robot's name, that crazy Scottish guy Abbott said, was "ARTHUR," and he announced it just like that, in a booming voice that put everything in capital letters: "AR-THUR!" I was standing beside Cory Yelland before Abbott snuck up behind us. Cory's my best friend, except he's a bit quieter and obviously a lot smarter than I am. "Don't look for trouble"—that's what Cory always said. My answer, of course, was always, "I don't have to look for trouble—it knows my address."

That much was for sure. Abbott had the two of us by the shoulder blades, showing off his creation to the class, and he gave me and Cory shakes all through his speech, harder than he probably meant to, urging all of us, "Say it! Can ye say it out loud, laddies? Say his name!"

"Arthur!" I answered, failing to stop my glasses from flying off as Abbott shook us. *"Arthur!"*

"What are yae yelling for, boy?" Abbott had already forgotten he'd grabbed me.

"My glasses flew off."

"Sorry."

"Tell him you've got some rare eye disease," whispered Cory. "Tell him if your glasses are broken, we're

2

talking major lawsuit, with one of those television lawyers with the spray-paint hair."

"Ah, they were loose anyway." I retrieved the glasses from the basement floor, undamaged for once, as Cory asked our crazy teacher, "What does 'Arthur' stand for?"

Abbott lived for questions like that. He was Scottish, his red hair long and tangled and streaked with wild gray, and except for shaving day, he was forever covered with three or four days of stubbly beard. This was not a shaving day. He ran to write quickly across his big white wipe board—it lined one corner of the basement—and his thick black pen whipped out the following sloppy words:

ARtificial life form created on THURsday.

"You're really reaching for names these days, eh?" This was from me.

"Mind your P's and Q's," said Abbott.

"Mind my what?"

"Forget it."

Time for some explanation. Abbott and Mrs. Abbott were science teachers at Abe Frohman Middle School, which is in Calpo, an Indiana town just a ways from Chicago. Being in seventh grade I had Mrs. Abbott, but I'd get Abbott for eighth and it would be a coin toss between them for ninth; they had once worked for NASA, had quit, and now had the Calpo science teaching market cornered.

A long-married pair of scientific misfits, they loved building things, especially robots, and although Arthur was the best yet, he was by no means the first; over the years

3

they'd produced several, and they kept them on display at school and in the lab at their house. The Abbotts were the first teachers I've ever had who took the class on field trips over the river and through the woods, down to their basement. It was a crackling October day, the week before Halloween; the weather was jacket cool but not quite freezing. The falling leaves were colored brown, orange, and red and stacking in yards I wanted to be out raking for fifteen dollars each, but I was ready to be just about anywhere: outside playing football or just prowling about. But no, there we were, twenty or so kids from seventh-grade science, crowded down there listening to the story of the Abbotts versus NASA.

They took turns relating bits of it and sounded more and more annoyed as the story went on, their faces growing red as they relived every setback and argument, Abbott with his Scottish brogue and babble, and Mrs. Abbott with her cold, point-by-point recitation; and if this is where they started to come across as a pair of mad scientists, I sure didn't notice at the time, because the stuff they were showing us was so cool.

They were showing us robots they'd built over the years.

Their first was called "Pig," and it sort of looked like a real pig, since it started out as a small vacuum cleaner, the kind you pull around by the hose, and they'd added about a gazillion different parts. "PIG" stood for *Position In Geosynch*, whatever that means. Pig's talent was finding walls. Switched on, Pig would crawl across a room until it bumped into something, then turn and crawl somewhere else.

Pig cost about $75,000 to build. I raised my hand to

say my hamster could do exactly the same things, and all he needed was shredded newspaper and two dollars' worth of hamster food, but the Abbotts had gone on to the next and weren't up for wise remarks anyway.

Pig went through a few improvements because it kept breaking, or finding walls it tried to push itself through instead of crawl around, and so they went on to build "MOUSE," which stood for *MOtorized Universally Sensitive Equipment*. Despite the name, Mouse was really just a bigger and more expensive version of Pig, but it not only crawled around things, it went over them, if possible, and could crawl over the rocks in the yard and the curbs on the street. Also, Mouse was fast—it whipped around the flat basement floor about ten times faster than Pig.

The Abbotts were sure that Mouse was going to crawl around the moon, but NASA sent astronauts instead, so they went on to the next step: "BEAST," *Better Equipped And Smarter Technology*. Beast was a Mouse with arms— six of them, in fact—although two seemed to be broken and Beast looked too much like a monster spider for anyone to be around without getting the screaming willies when it moved.

Since the moon had already been done, Beast was supposed to go to the planet Mars and prowl around for Martians and rocks, but it wasn't ready in time, so NASA sent the Viking spacecraft instead, and now the Abbotts were *really* mad at the government space agency. So they took a shot, said Mrs. Abbott, "And crossed a new and improved Beast with a Loser."

Sandy Miller asked the question this time—Sandy, with the always perfect blond hair and pointed nose. Sandy

5

from row three, one from the aisle, nine and a half feet from where I sat, not that I ever noticed; this was Sandy who hated me. "Why would you cross your robot with a loser?"

"LOSER," said Mrs. Abbott. "A *Local Operating System Equipped to Roam.*"

"A brain on wheels," said Abbott, giving his wife a pat on the back. She was the one who'd invented it, and he let her explain. "Loser was better than just a computer; it was supposed to actually *think*, have these same sort of conversations with itself that we all do, such as, 'Okay, now if I've bumped into the wall, and I know there are four walls, and the only way out of this basement is the steps, then there's no point in bumping into all of the walls before I move toward the steps because—' "

"Ow!" I interrupted, holding my head and being a wiseguy. "I hate story problems. 'If a train leaves Indianapolis at two P.M. going north at fifty miles an hour, and there are thirty people on board, and sixteen of them jump off the back holding seven oranges and two lemons each while the train is going up a hill . . .' "

"Arthur has cost nearly three million dollars to build," said Abbott, going on.

"Wow," I said, "I didn't know teaching paid that well."

Mrs. Abbott frowned, giving me that look again. "We've had a number of important grants that have enabled us to continue our research."

"Wow again," I said. "Can I get this grant guy's phone number? Maybe he'll enable me to continue my comic book collection."

6

Sandy's hand went up. Ignoring me, as always, she asked, "How smart will Arthur be when he's switched on?"

"Very smart. His two brains include a high-speed computer. We've programmed his backup brain with incredible abilities, an encyclopedia of knowledge. He'll be able to call upon this information when needed."

"Two brains?"

"Yes. We want him to be as human as possible, and everyone here has two brains."

Making the obvious point, I said, "I've only got one brain."

"I didn't know you had *that* many," said Sandy. She turned to Mrs. Abbott, saying, "What do you mean, everybody has two brains?"

"Well, it's actually one brain with two major parts. Part of your brain is automatic; it controls your breathing, your heartbeat, and your internal organs. You don't have to remember to breathe, right? If you touch your finger to something very hot, it jerks away automatically; you don't have to think about that, either. That's one of your brains, and Arthur has one of those as well."

I stared at the robot. It was ugly, and it got uglier the more attention Sandy paid to it. Another bad thing. Besides, it was off, not working, and about as entertaining to watch as the lawnmower in Dad's garage.

"Not that it matters, but what's the other brain used for?"

"Higher functions. Thinking, learning, making decisions. It's the higher brain functions that separate people from animals. When perfected, Arthur will be like us, only

7

better. We've programmed his backup brain with extraordinary knowledge. He'll be able to call upon this information when needed. Virtually indestructible, he'll be able to walk through fire and suffer extreme cold without minding; he won't even need to breathe, so we could send him into space—"

"Not for NASA," said Abbott, very stubborn. Abbott had a big beef with NASA.

"Well, maybe for somebody," said Mrs. Abbott. "A lot of people will be going to space over the next few years, and Arthur will be there."

"If he's perfected."

"He'll be perfected."

"Aye, eventually."

I was taking a closer look at this mechanical kid. "He looks like he'll be pretty strong."

"Aye, strong enough. He could lift a car over his head and balance it for a while."

"Could he throw it?"

"Why would we be wanting to throw cars around, boy?"

"Just wondered." I could imagine myself as being that strong, some sort of cyborg—half-person, half–robot warrior—fighting for justice, just like in the comic books. "He could be a superhero," I said, the idea getting me excited. "Forget about sending him into space. You could program him to fight crime and search out evil. There's lots he could do. This basement could be his secret hiding place, and—"

I stopped talking. Half the class was staring at me,

8

Sandy Miller especially, and so were the Abbotts. "Just an idea," I said. "I'm an idea guy."

It was time to leave, and they started to pack us all up. The class was counted to see if anyone was missing and then everybody started back up the stairs. I was following when I felt that hand on my shoulder again.

"Hold up, boy."

Me and my big mouth. I was in trouble and knew it, but this didn't stop me from trying to talk my way out of detention. "I just asked questions, I just wanted to know more about this Arthur thing, and I didn't mean anything bad by it—"

"Easy; we know," said Mrs. Abbott, backing her husband off and giving me some room. "Take it easy."

"Okay."

Sizing me up, Abbott said, "You've an interest in robots, don't you, lad?"

I thought about it and shrugged. "I like the idea of having a machine buddy around who could bail me out of trouble."

"A good buddy," said Abbott.

"Yeah."

"What about the best of buddies?"

"Huh?"

Abbott didn't explain, not yet. He said, "It's just that you seemed so interested, we want to show you a couple of things about Arthur that . . . well, most of the class wouldn't understand."

"Oh, yeah?" This impressed me, since I was never one of the smartest kids in class. Maybe I had a knack for this robot thing. Maybe I could wind up working for NASA

9

someday myself. Maybe I'd invent something so radical that I'd get in a fight with the bigshots, too.

"And the real important fact is, we need a favor from you."

"A favor, from *me*? What do you need?"

Important point: when adults start asking favors of thirteen-year-olds, nothing real good can possibly happen.

The Abbotts linked arms and walked me over, saying, "Let's look at Arthur first, give you the real scoop."

The real scoop. So they showed me the robot again, and I was still impressed. I even asked a question: "Why haven't you turned him on yet?"

Abbott answered thoughtfully, saying, "Because once he's switched on, he can't be switched off."

"Why not?"

"We didn't build him with an off switch, and we did it on purpose. We want him to be as human as possible, and think about it, Max: how would you like it if you had an off switch and everybody knew where it was?"

Good point. I'd spend a lot of time "off" and parked in the closet at home, I figured, especially when Mom was gone and Dad's basketball games were on.

"It's a question of system integrity," Abbott was explaining. "The new type of computer intelligence we've developed—the higher-function brain—is in the early stages. Only certain frequencies of brain-wave activity can be replicated. Adult brain waves won't work—that's why Mrs. Abbott and I can't be used. We need a boy, laddie, a bright boy to help us finish the experiment."

I was getting a cold, scary feeling now. "Uh . . .

10

yeah, right,'' I said to the Abbotts, backing away as I spoke. "So what exactly is it that you guys want from me?''

It was the Mrs. who answered, and her smile made me shudder. "Max, we need to borrow your brain . . .''

2

EX-SQUEEZE ME?

Borrow my brain?

That's the sort of thing which makes a person back up a bit, and I kept backing up. "Uh, I'd love to let you have my brain, that's got to be good for extra credit, right? But the thing of it is, I'm sort of using it right now."

And I was—I was using it to try and figure out which way I was going to run and how loud I was going to scream.

Mrs. Abbott saw that, though, and spoke to calm me down. "Oh, no, no, Max—you don't understand. We don't want to hurt you."

Yeah, right. "I bet cutting out my brain would hurt just a little bit."

They both pretended to be shocked. "Who said anything about cutting out your brain?"

"You guys just said you wanted to borrow it."

"Bad choice of words, lad," said Abbott. "What we want to do is *copy* it."

"Copy it?"

"Copy your brain. It will be like making a duplicate of a tape recording—same process. What we want to do is copy the good stuff from inside your brain and give it to Arthur."

"We've programmed incredible bits of knowledge into Arthur, but we're concerned about balance," explained Mrs. Abbott. "The human mind is so complex it can't really be duplicated—unless you actually duplicate one."

"Uh-huh." My heart wasn't beating quite so fast now, but I still had no idea what these guys were talking about. Except that they wanted to run my brain through a copy machine or something.

"Would it hurt?" I asked.

"You won't even know it's happening."

"This is too weird."

"Science is weird, lad. When the Wright brothers stood poised with that first aeroplane, what do you think their neighbors were saying at Kitty Hawk? They were saying, 'There go those weird Wright boys with a funny-looking kite.' "

"And what about Einstein?" asked Mrs. Abbott, playing along. "That big-time scientist scribbling so much nonsense on a blackboard and never tying his shoelaces?"

"Weird?" I asked.

"A complete *wacko*," answered Abbott. "But that's neither here nor there; we need your brainpower, boy. Would you let us have some? Do you have the courage?"

"What do you mean, courage?"

13

"Are you brave enough?"

"Brave enough . . . I guess, if I knew for what."

"The for–what's are all going to come in time. All you have to do is be bold. We're doing new and important things."

"New and important?" I suddenly *felt* important. It was a tingling feeling, as if I was the center of everything, and I was definitely the center of *their* attention. "Yes," they said. "Your name will be remembered alongside the great ones of science history, like . . . like that guy who walked on the moon."

"You mean Neil Armstrong?"

"Yes, him."

"Wow," I said, but I still couldn't see how a kid's name was ever going to be up there with the great ones of history. Come to think of it, how many kids have ever been famous for anything other than not cleaning their rooms?

So back to the question: Was I brave?

Time would tell.

The Abbotts made some fast arrangements. We went upstairs and they gave me a cold drink and set me in a chair long enough to send the rest of the field-tripping class back to school. They packed off the teachers and parents and kids with smiles and held me back with barely an explanation other than, "We need to bring back Maxwell in our own manner."

Which nobody questioned. All I can say is, it was a good thing the Abbotts planned nothing worse for me than a bit of brain stealing.

14

Next they called my mom and dad and told them I was involved in some terrific afterschool extra-credit project that was sure to get me into Harvard or Yale or some other college I was never going to be able to afford, and this made Mom and Dad happy beyond belief, although I think they said they'd be right over to watch, because Mrs. Abbott said into the phone, "Why, certainly, that sounds like a fine, fine idea. Let me give you our address and directions; do you know where Old Pine Road is?"

Apparently not. Mrs. Abbott explained some turns and landmarks and other directions, then she did another one of those mad scientist–type things right in front of me: she lied, saying, "Well, yes, but he really can't come to the phone just right now. Max is helping Mr. Abbott set up the experiment."

"No, I'm not," I started to say. "I'm standing here—"

Mrs. Abbott held up a finger for silence and got off the phone quickly, leading me back downstairs and saying to her husband, "Time is a minor issue, Thomas." They huddled and she explained what had happened.

"Why did you give them directions?" Abbott was whispering now, as if I couldn't hear.

"What else was I supposed to do? Not tell them? I gave them the longest possible route, and besides, nothing will go wrong and they can get the little brat out of our hair while we work with Arthur."

Little brat? *"Hey,"* I started to say. *"What's the big idea . . . ?"*

"Right," said Mr. Abbott, grabbing me by the shoulders for a more in-depth tour of the lab. "What we're going

15

to try here has never been attempted, you know. There's not much room for error. If you make an omelet and muck up the works, you call it scrambled eggs. But this—''

''Scrambled brains?''

Abbott grinned. ''Not quite that bad, but you see the point, don't you, laddie? It's serious work that we're about.''

Omelets, scrambled eggs, and my central nervous system . . . that's what I was thinking about as Abbott and his wife danced around the basement lab, getting ready to hitch me up to their robot, except I got distracted by checking out the actual robot himself. *Itself,* I guess, except it—*he*—seemed so much more of a real thing than Pig, or Mouse, or Beast, or whatever other nonsense the Abbotts might have slapped together.

I almost felt sorry for that silent robot kid. He was like the Scarecrow in *The Wizard of Oz,* after all; all he wanted was a brain. That sort of made the Abbotts just as much like the Scarecrow, though; all *they* wanted was a brain, too.

Mine.

These people were about to be messing around with my brain. Maybe I *should* run this by my mom and dad before I let the Abbotts start doing anything drastic. They were on their way over, right? All I needed to do was stall.

The Abbotts weren't much for stalling. ''Lie back on the table,'' Mrs. Abbott said.

Table. Mr. Abbott had reclined Arthur the silent robot back on a workbench and slid a second workbench up beside it. Between the two was some more rolling equipment with cables and wires and such; it was as if they were going to give a car battery a jump off another. "That's almost what we're about," agreed Abbott when I said this. "We're almost going to jump Arthur off your brain."

"Well, don't take too much brain juice," I said, trying to stall for time. "I haven't got all that much to spare— you guys know that. Think about my grades. I'm barely passing."

"Passing? You're not passing," said Abbott.

"Well, there you go," I said, slapping my forehead. "It's worse than I thought. I think I should—"

Both Abbotts took hold and boosted me up on the table without waiting for permission. "Lie back. This will help your grade," Abbott said.

"Right." I did, but almost immediately changed my mind: *forget this, this is crazy.* Except I didn't get a chance to complain, because before I could stand up, they strapped me down. Two big straps across my chest, two on the legs, two on each arm. "Hey, what's going on?"

"We have to restrain your movements," said Abbott, that crazy Scot. He was right in my face, looking as big as a balloon, breathing on me, and his laugh was . . . well, mad. "We don't want you to move at all, boy."

"Why not?"

"We want to restrict unnecessary brain waves. If you're flopping about, those brain commands could drown out the thinking side, and that's the portion we want to copy."

"Sorry," I said. "I've never had my brain copied before."

"*No one* has ever had his brain copied before."

Mrs. Abbott started whipping out white tape and in a

17

flash she had me connected to the big metal black machine box between me and the robot. She switched on what looked like a bunch of Christmas lights. The scariest bit of the setup, though, was the big red switch, which looked like the sort of thing that controlled the electric chair in those old prison movies.

"Commence primary ignition," ordered Mrs. Abbott.

Click, slap, ka-chunk! All I caught was a blur of shaggy red hair as Abbott slammed everything together. That's also when I heard him laughing again.

This was all scary and getting scarier. I was strapped flat to a table next to Arthur the robot, and the Abbotts were buzzing back and forth between us, adjusting connections and dials and switches. They even turned off most of the basement lights, "To avoid a short circuit or power outage," said Mrs. Abbott, but that just cast the whole thing in dark shadow, making it look more and more like something out of a horror movie.

"Uh," I said, "I think I remember this scene from *Frankenstein*. Aren't you guys strapping me in like the monster?"

"Set the secondary sensors," ordered Mrs. Abbott.

There I was, strapped in, my heart pounding. The connections to my head were itching like crazy, and I didn't know whether that was just because I was starting to sweat underneath the white tape or because the Abbotts were zapping voltage already.

Thump! Mrs. Abbott threw a switch and the table beneath me began to shudder from the vibrations of some enormous piece of machinery in that basement.

18

"Now!" screamed Mrs. Abbott.

Abbott slammed down on the big red button.

"Ahhhhhh!" There was a loud scream, and as everything went black, I realized the person screaming was me . . .

[3]

UGH

When I opened my eyes, the first thing I noticed was this: they weren't my eyes.

Mr. and Mrs. Abbott were both standing over me, one on each side of the table. Mrs. Abbott looked as white as a ghost, and she didn't even appear to be breathing, but Abbott popped out with that crazy laugh again, crazier than before, even, and he said, "It . . . is . . . *alive!*"

Huh? *What?* "I better be alive," I said, "or you guys are going to be in a lot of trouble when my mom and dad get here."

Mrs. Abbott did a quick fade then; I thought she was fainting, but she came back with a video camera and started making a tape of me lying there. "Say something," she said. "Speak to us."

"Wha . . . what happened?" I couldn't sit up, of course, because I was strapped down, but when I rocked my head to the left I saw myself, my own unconscious body, lying strapped down on the table next to me.

Impossible.

"That's me . . ." I said.

"Arthur . . ." Abbott was patting me on the head, and my head rattled as if it was made of metal. Wait a minute: my head *was* made of metal, and Mrs. Abbott was saying, "Arthur, look at me. You have been activated."

"Activated? What are you talking about, Mrs. Abbott? I'm *Max*. This is *me*. You guys have *really messed up*."

"Complete memory mapping," whispered Mr. Abbott, as he stepped over beside his wife. "Amazing."

"It's not amazing," I said. "It's making me mad. Let me up from here!"

"In a few moments . . ." said Mrs. Abbott, also speaking in a whisper from behind her camera. She looked at her husband and back over to where my body lay, blinking.

This was not a good thing, I thought, but then something flashed in my head like lightning in the middle of the night, zapping my attention, and part of it was:

YSTEM REBOOT CHEC
IFIED EMERGENCY BACKU
000111222 BINA
UUII;;PPPP

And just seeing all that in a quick second hurt. It actually, really *hurt,* making me jerk my head back to make it go away, but that was when I realized the pain I was feeling was . . . well, it was the same sort of pain I might feel if I ate a cold ice cream cone too fast, that ice cream

21

headache, except the headache went away the very second I jolted back from the flashing lightning I was seeing.

I was experiencing this completely alien, mechanical feeling, and it was just about enough to make me crazy.

"What did you guys do to me?"

"We have created you, laddie," said Abbott, all smiles, looking like a guy who just won an award or something. "We've brought you alive into the world this day. This is more than we could ever have hoped for."

"What are you talking about, man? You guys better let me up and out of here, or you're going to be in real trouble."

"'Tis so perfect . . ." Abbott was whispering.

Mrs. Abbott just kept taping me.

"You think I'm the robot? Listen, you boneheads, you've messed up and switched my brain into the machine. I'm Max, Max Helvey. Idea guy. Ask me anything. Oh, boy, is this a bad thing."

"It's a *good* thing," said Abbott. "You've been created whole cloth from where once there was nothing but raw elements: metal, wiring, circuitry. It will take you some time to absorb your programming."

"My *what?*"

"Your secondary systems are rebooting from the shutdown. That'll take you a few moments to understand."

"What? I—"

INTEGER REJEC
PSYCHOSYMBIOSIS ALT
DOS 8.8 EXEC.PRE

"Ahhhh!" That screeching pain again, along with the lightning-quick flash of computer stuff in my head, and what had these weird weasels done to me, anyway? I was getting scared but realized then why my heart wasn't pounding from fear.

It was because I didn't have a heart anymore. These maniacs had moved my brain into their stupid robot.

"Put me back!" I said then, starting to panic. "Turn your stupid machine on and put me back inside my body, where I belong!"

"Easy," said the Abbotts.

"No," I said, doing my best to glare, but not knowing how to work this guy's face yet. "This is not easy, this is hard. Hard—and bad," I said, speaking as slowly and calmly as I could manage. "So put me back now, please."

Instead, they just stared down at me and taped.

Okay, I thought in an angry moment. *I can deal with this; I can deal with this long enough to convince them they've made the biggest mistake of their whole building-robots-in-the-basement lives.*

I took stock and tried to figure out exactly what I was right now, and one of the first things I noticed was that I was suddenly aware of my blinking.

Think about it: *blinking* is one of those things people do all the time, constantly, and they never notice it, but I did—*click-click, click-click.* Two back-to-back blinks every thirty seconds, closing my eyesight down on a regular schedule.

Obviously, the backup brain I was tied into didn't work as well as the Abbotts thought it did, and why was I blinking in the first place? It was purely to make the robot

23

seem alive, more normal, because the blinks weren't keeping the eyes clean and moist, like they do on real people—the blinks were just blinks.

Click-click, click-click . . .

If I was going to be stuck in this body for any time at all, that was going to have to stop, and I figured out I had the power. By concentrating, I could tell the eyes not to open and shut like that, and I turned them off.

Click-click, click . . .

No more blinking.

Well, that was one thing. But I wanted my body back—*now!*

Then, in a sudden moment, I heard my own voice being spoken by somebody else: *me.*

The robot brain that was now in my body was speaking to the Abbotts, saying, "Uh, folks? I'd like to get out of here now."

"What?" This was from me, and I looked over at myself and said, "Listen Arthur, or Hal, or whoever or whatever you think you are, you're not fooling me. They messed up and you think you're cool now, but you just wait."

"Abbott—Mrs. Abbott—please." The thing in my body was looking at me with wide eyes now, all right; he knew I meant business. "This is not a good thing," he was saying, "and I'd like to get up from here."

Except they were believing him—*it*—and not me.

This robot who was in my body was playing it cool, and he was saying, "Mr. Abbott, I'm scared."

"Easy boy, easy . . ." They were unstrapping him.

"Wait," I said, pulling tight the straps that were holding

24

me down. "What are you doing, letting him go? He's got my body; don't just let him get up and run out of here."

"Arthur, be silent a moment." This was from Mr. Abbott, and he sounded less like the mad scientist and more like my dad when he's annoyed.

"My name's not Arthur," I said. "It's Max, Max Helvey, and—"

Abbott gave me just a quick glance. "You're confused for now. We'll have to adjust your programming."

"His programming?" said Mrs. Abbott, speaking from behind her camera.

"Just a bug, a glitch, no big problem."

"Uh-uh," I said. "This is a *big* problem, Mr. Abbott."

"Don't make me say it again," he said.

"Why? Are you going to send me to bed without my oilcan?"

From somewhere in the basement there was a noise then, a *buzzzzzz* that indicated someone was upstairs, because Mrs. Abbott put down the camera and scampered upstairs while Abbott and that robot creep in my body both stared at me like I was a turtle in a jar.

"This isn't funny," I said. "You wait until I get out of here, you little rat creep. I'll—"

I shut up then; what was I going to do? Beat myself up? This was crazy.

"His parents are here," Mrs. Abbott announced, reappearing at the top of the steps.

What? *Mom and Dad?*

"Get me out of here! *Mom! Mom! Dad!*" I started screaming, but at the same time, so did that robot dude in my body, and he sounded a lot more like me than I did.

He was shouting at the top of his lungs—*my* lungs—
"Mommy!"

Mommy? I hadn't called Mom that in years, but if it was good enough for my robot buddy, it was good enough for me, and by the time Mom and Dad appeared at the top of the basement steps, racing down, we were both screaming it as loud as we could, and the whole thing was a horrible scene.

Now, my Dad's no rocket scientist or robot-building maniac, he's a regular person—a transmission guy. I've heard the stories a zillion times. After getting out of the Marine Corps in Oklahoma, he started out as a box packer at a canned foods factory, worked his way up just far enough to realize there was no such way as "up" there, and so then went to school to learn auto repair. From there he worked for people for a long while before realizing the best thing in life is to have people work for you, so he took a chance, got some lucky breaks, and wound up with his own pair of transmission shops, one in Calpo, a second in Michigan City, and another on the way.

Business was confusing, Dad always said, and he always seemed to tag it with, "I've built a monster, I've built myself a monster . . ."

Not quite as bad as the monster the Abbotts slapped together, I thought.

"Great Scot," said my father, looking startled.

"Welcome," said Abbott, moving to intercept him. "I'm sorry about the chaos, but it seems our little experiment has gone a bit *too* perfectly."

"What?" My father was concerned and angry, and Mom looked as if she was ready to crack a chair across somebody's teeth as the Abbotts tried to explain just what it was that had happened.

"What is *that?*" exclaimed my father, holding Mom back from running over to me, the silver-skinned robot lying on the slab. "What have you been doing down here?"

"It's a long story," said Abbott, starting to lurch into it. "You see, once we worked for NASA, the National Aeronautics and Space Administration—"

"What?"

"And we constructed our first robot, called Pig—"

"What are you people talking about?" demanded my father. "What are you people doing with my son wired up to that . . . that *thing?*"

I was the thing, and I started to say it very loudly, but nobody was hearing me.

We argued over which of us was the real Max, but Mom and Dad didn't seem to be questioning this at all. They were wrapping their arms around that creep in my body.

Giving me just the faintest hope that he was at least thinking things over, Mr. Abbott said, "Perhaps it might be best to keep Max overnight with us until we've checked out his condition further . . ."

"You must be crazy," said Dad. "You'll be lucky if you don't see us in court."

"We'll *sue*!" said Mom.

I wouldn't call my mother one of those elegant people on the planet, but she sets records for decent; I don't think my mother ever yelled at the cat or dog, much less my brother or me. And not because she was timid—I once

27

saw my mom screeching in the face of a state highway patrol officer as he tried to write her a ticket she thought wasn't justified.

Mom's a tolerant, nice person, but even she has her limits. That cop saw it, and so did the Abbotts, although they tried to change her mind.

"I *do* wish you'd reconsider . . ."

"We're not about to risk our son."

Their son? I kept yelling, "That's not your son, Mom—*I'm* your son! Please don't leave me down here with these wackos! Wait!"

Only, they weren't waiting; Mom and Dad were leaving, and they were leaving with that robot who'd stolen my body.

No way. I wasn't going to let that happen, so I started stretching again, pulling against the straps, and the Abbotts were staring at me, just like this kid Billy Costello once had when he'd tried to beat me up over my lunch money. Well, I wasn't wimping out for an Abbott *or* a Costello, and what I flashed on now was:

STRENGTH OVERPULL—EXCESSIVE
TORQUE STRESS FACTOR
CENTERALITY MAGNIFICA

Except *this* time, I didn't feel any shock or pain. *This* time I accessed that silly computer inside my head and it worked the way I guess it was supposed to, because suddenly I had the strength and power of ten or twenty people, and this time when I sat up on that bench I wasn't held

28

back; this time it was as if the straps binding me were made of soft spaghetti, or nothing at all, because they popped like shoelaces.

Mrs. Abbott screamed.

"You guys aren't keeping me here," I said, rising. "My mom and dad don't know what you did, or who that creep inside my body is, but I know. *I* know!"

"Stop him!" Mrs. Abbott was screaming.

"I will," said Abbott, trying to block my path.

I pushed him out of the way and was shocked at how fast he flew and bounced off the wall, stunned. "You're acting like a monster!" he screamed.

"I'm not a monster! I'm Max—"

Mrs. Abbott didn't believe me, either, and she yelled, "You're a beast and must be stopped!"

"Nobody's stopping me; I've got your robot kid's super body! Why don't you get your stupid camera and tape this?" I knocked the table back over and it collapsed with a loud bang, and I would have ripped their lab apart except that as stupid as I was, I realized they were going to need their equipment in order to put me back in my body. So instead, I just scrambled past the Abbotts, and since they had the steps blocked off, climbed up the wall, broke out the glass, and escaped through the shattered basement window into the early evening . . .

4

ESCAPE

Clump-clump, clump-clump . . .

As I ran, I realized right away that although I was strong, I wasn't very fast. Also, this robot's feet didn't seem to lift and fall the same way as a real person's feet—or like *my* old feet, anyway. I sounded like a horse galloping. *Terrific.*

It was getting dark outside, and cold, but I knew it was cold more because I could just sense the temperature than out of any actual feeling. I mean, I wasn't uncomfortable; I didn't feel cold; I just *knew* it was cold. The robot body I was trapped in wasn't breathing, so there was no fog of breath to see.

And I could see really well—*incredibly* well. These new robot eyes could see in lots of different ways that real eyes couldn't. If I wanted, I could squint and suddenly see infrared, for one thing—night vision that let me see light and heat sources; I could sense things ahead in the dark better than any cat.

30

I could see long distances; how far, I wondered? I tried concentrating on something my mind was telling me, which was:

RANGEFINDER TRACKING
XXP 10 XXP 20 XXP 30 XXP 40
IMUM TARGET ACQUISITION

Except now when I concentrated, I could see more of a field of vision, seeing the world through a computer screen that said:

ACCESS MINIMUM TARGET ACQUISITION CRITERIA—
SORT TARGET—SELECT   !
—!—
!
INDICATED TARGETING (MARK XXXX)

This time I could do it. *Man* . . .

And as before, there was no pain; the sting was just a click now, like changing directions on an electronic game.

That was it, I realized. My brain was like a Nintendo set, or a GameBoy, or something like that; all I needed to do was change cartridges. And there was a list posted in there of all the things I could do, all my capabilities, if I wanted to, among which were:

RANGEFINDER
TRACKING/DETECTION
MONITOR/RECORD

SYSTEM RESOURCES
TELECOMMUNICATIONS ACCESS
EXTERNAL COM CHATTER
HOMEBASE RELAY
DATABASE ACCESS/ASSESSMENT

Telecommunications access, I read, and in that instant I realized I could listen in on phone calls, discovering this after another sudden jolt, another of those flashes, this one reading:

EXTERNAL COM CHATTER—TELECOMMUNICATION
DETECT
IMMEDIATE VICINITY ON LOCAL FREQUENCY
MONITOR?

Monitor? I thought, just wondering what all that meant, but the mere thought told the secondary brain—the big computer inside me—that I did want to monitor the telecommunication it was sensing, the phone call, and immediately I could hear Mrs. Abbott on the phone with someone, and she was yelling—not screaming, just yelling—and what she was saying was, "Well, you had better do *something* fast, Lieutenant, because this is an emergency."

The voice on the other end was that of a military type, very crisp, all business. "Stand by one, Ma'am, because I don't understand—"

Mrs. Abbott cracked it out slow and steady. "Our cover is blown here, Lieutenant. You're the duty officer, and there's been a major, major malfunction and we need backup fast."

"I'll need you to authenticate, Dr. Abbott. You know I just can't take a flash precedence call without—"

"Yes, yes, all right. Hold on, I've got that silly card somewhere around here and—here it is. I authenticate alpha delta delta X ray seven. Okay? All right, then?"

"Stand by one," said the voice. Then: "Authentication is valid. So what exactly is the problem, Dr. Abbott?"

"Project Prometheus, that's the problem. Arthur the robot? He's up and out, and he's got a temper."

"Your crazy robot project?"

"Yes, our crazy robot project. It attacked my husband and tore up our lab and it's out there racing through the woods and ready to destroy everything in its path."

What? That was a lie; I wasn't going to destroy anything.

The military guy on the other end took a deep breath and said, "You cannot be serious."

"I am serious."

"I'll say this much. You've gone too far this time, Dr. Abbott—you and your husband have gone *way* too far."

"Don't you think I know that now? But fire us later. Right now there's a monster in the Calpo woods, and you'd better do something about it."

"I'll send out some alert search teams, but I'm going to need more details."

"The details are in your computer files. What more do you want from me? You'd better do something fast."

"I intend to, Dr. Abbott. And when we find your robot, we'll destroy it for you."

33

Destroy it? Destroy me?

This was *not* a good thing. Nope.

"Wait a minute," said the military guy. "We can't talk about this on an insecure line. Let's go to scrambler."

Screeeeeeeeech! Something clicked on the telephones, and all of a sudden I couldn't hear either of them anymore. All I got was some crazy loud screeching noise—scrambled, I guess—but it wasn't too difficult to figure out what Dr. Abbott and her military buddy were talking about.

Me.

I knew the truth now, anyway. The Abbotts didn't just have the Calpo science market cornered. They were there on purpose, working on the robot projects for some secret government agency, and now they'd made a mistake, and I was caught up in it, a brain without a body.

I needed to get moving; I needed to get home somehow and talk to Mom and Dad. If I got the chance to explain myself, to tell them just what had happened with my brain in the lab, then everything would be all right. Then we could do something.

So I was a fugitive, running through the woods, trying to head back toward town, to find my parents and convince them of the truth before it was too late.

Walking through the woods at night was strange, spooky. The moon was full, so there was plenty of light for my night vision system to help me see with, and I was amazed at how many things were alive and about in the woods; I'd never known that northern Indiana was such of a wilderness.

I saw a raccoon and it saw me, meeting my gaze with its glowing eyes as it stood on a rock for a moment, waving its front paws in challenge before scampering away.

Then my light sensors saw a light deep in the woods, a flickering fire light, and I headed toward it.

There was a bearded, sort of scrungy-looking guy in an Army jacket tending a fire, cooking something out of a can he'd scraped into a tiny pot. Nearby was a bedroll, with a sheet or tarp of some kind anchored to a tree in order to break the wind.

"Well, hello there," he said, looking up. If he was shocked to see a big robot kid stumble into his little camp he barely showed it; maybe his eyebrows went up a bit. "Nice night for a hike," he said.

"I . . . I'm not hiking," I said. "I'm running away from some people."

He offered me up his little pot. "Are you hungry?"

I stared at the food and realized that I could smell it, and the food smelled good, but I had no appetite. It was as if I'd just eaten a big meal and was full. Then I figured out why: it was because I was a machine.

Except thinking about food equals energy, and just by thinking about it I found that I could access the information on my robot power, because it all flashed:

SYSTEM RESOURCES
submenu—Power [Batteries]
Power [Internal Generation—OFFLINE]
Power [Access—OFFLINE]

Then:

SUBMENU—POWER [BATTERIES]
Battery power at 34% of full charge
Significant Drain—Undetermined Cause
Remaining Power: 39 Hours

Thirty-nine hours.

I was no rocket scientist, but I realized if I didn't solve my power problem within thirty-nine hours, I was going to run out of energy and shut down.

Then what happened? Did that mean I'd die? Or just hibernate, like some bear sitting out the winter?

The guy by the fire offered me some food again, saying, "Go ahead and eat something. Don't worry about me. I've got another can."

"That's okay," I said. "I'm not hungry."

"Suit yourself." He produced a spoon and ate straight from the pot for a while before saying, "Do you mind if I ask you a question?"

"Go ahead."

"Are you from outer space?"

"Huh?" I realized what he meant, though. The silver of the robot skin was shining in the moonlight; I must have looked like something that had just stepped out of a flying saucer. *Take me to your leader,* I thought, but didn't say. I said, "No. I'm from Calpo."

He looked at me funny. "What part of town?"

"Just in town. I don't usually look like this."

"Uh-huh. So what are you? Some sort of machine?"

"Sort of," I said. "These crazy people stole my brain from my body and stuck it in a robot, so now I'm running around trying to get home so I can get my body back."

He nodded, licking his spoon. "Yeah. That happened to me once."

"Really?"

"No." He changed his mind, shaking his head. "No, not really. Thought I'd say something to make you feel better."

"Thanks."

"You got a name?"

"Max Helvey," I said.

"Hey, Max. I'm Walter."

"What are you doing out here, Walter?"

He shrugged. "Just being a lonely guy. You know how it is."

"I guess so." I was feeling pretty lonely myself.

"Is the Army looking for you?"

"I don't know."

"Those look like Army choppers."

"Huh?"

He pointed and I looked up, and that, I realized, was the buzzing sound I'd been hearing: helicopters. Three of them, with searchlights, flying around over the woods with their lights aimed down. Far from us, but getting closer . . . *fast*.

"Oh, no!" I said, jumping up. Except, there was no place to go.

The lonely guy nodded at his tarp. "Lie over there and I'll cover you up. Better move fast."

I saw what he meant; one of the low-flying helicopters was swooping toward us at barely treetop level. I crawled down to the ground and the lonely guy casually pulled his tarp down so it completely covered me like a blanket.

37

I could see out some, just enough to watch the lonely guy's campsite become as bright as day with the glow of several searchlights from above, the leaves flying around as his fire crackled and sparked under the whipping winds of the helicopters' rotor blades. The lonely guy took the light in his face, giving the pilots a wave, and after a few really scary minutes the aircraft flew off and the camp was dark again, except for the small glow of the fire.

"It's clear now," he said, and I crawled out from underneath the tarp, thanking him. "Ah, that's okay," he said. "Only problem is, my spoon got knocked into the fire."

I saw it there, sitting between some bits of flickering wood, so I reached into the burning fire and pulled out the spoon, blowing on it so it would be cool and not burn his hand. "Thanks a lot," he said.

"No problem."

"Good luck to you."

"Thanks," I said, getting up to move on. I figured I was going to need all the luck I could get . . .

5

SANCTUARY?

Somewhere in the distance, a bunch of dogs had started barking and howling.

Wonderful. For all I knew, they had the sheriff and his boys following me with a pack of bloodhounds, just like in the old prison escape movies. Except that didn't make sense—what could the dogs be smelling? What kind of scent could a robot leave, besides the lingering aroma of lubricating oil?

Wouldn't those silly dogs wind up chasing a bunch of Toyotas instead of me?

"Can't take the chance," I said out loud. It was silly to talk, but I was lonely, so excuse me for living—check that thought; I was a robot. Excuse me for operating to peak performance.

Trying to get my bearings, I accessed the internal compass inside the computer brain—an overly functional compass gyroscope thing that told me I was headed north, as well as a lot of silly things such as wind speed and direction, how negotiable the terrain was considered, and the pack and dew content of the ground. It also gave a few other pointless numbers such as the barometric pressure and my sensitivity to comm chatter—the communications going around me.

"A lot of which doesn't make sense in a weasel's world," I said out loud. The joke I'll explain later, the thing of my thought was, why would the Abbotts build their robot with so many strange functions and abilities if they were just going to shoot it into outer space? The robot my brain was stuck in would have made a better tracker in an old western movie than an astronaut. If I was even half understanding what I was seeing, then I'd have a better chance of tracking the dogs than they would have of tracking me.

So, figuring out how all that nonsense worked, that was how I once again tripped into overhearing some comm chatter between the people who'd built me—the Abbotts—and the people out looking for me—the Army.

Mrs. Abbott was on a cellular phone, saying, "I don't have a scrambler for my car phone, Captain, because you people wouldn't pay for one—Remember? *Remember?*"

"I'm sorry, Ma'am, but I don't think we should be discussing this on an insecure channel."

"Nobody *cares* what you think, Captain Sellers—that *is* your name, isn't it? So have you killed that thing yet? We're the ones on the hook here. You're the one who's supposed to be helping us solve this problem."

"We're working on it. I've authorized every resource . . ."

"What about the stealth choppers? The robot choppers? Have you released them?"

"*Mrs. Abbott,*" said the captain sternly, "there are some things we absolutely cannot talk about, and if you keep this up, I'll hang up the telephone."

Robot stealth choppers? This fell into the category of bad things, I thought. It was potentially a terribly bad thing.

"I worked on that project, Captain Sellers, and the only reason it's Top Secret is because I made it Top Secret, and I know how vicious and powerful those things are, so open up your silly little airplane hangars and send them out. *They're killer bees from outer space! We designed those robot helos to be killer bees from outer space!* So don't just sit there; send them out to get Arthur! *Send them!* Send them out now, or else—"

Click! *Beeeepppp . . . !*

One person or the other hung up, because the telephone call in my ears went away to a loud beep noise and I shut it off, and since worrying about robot helicopters or killer bees from space didn't make much sense (obviously this was the computer side of the brain putting its two cents in—the kid side was ready to start screaming for Mom), I tried to worry instead about the main problem.

Where was I? The woods were thinning out now, and I was edging my way back into Calpo, coming up behind the houses that marked our end of town. There were lights, and car noises, and a few barking dogs, but nothing like a panic, or anything. Nobody was looking for a crazed robot out here, anyway.

I crawled into a backyard, slipping through loose planks

41

of a big redwood fence, and was staring at the house, thinking how much I needed to try and call home, try and talk to Mom and Dad and reason with them. The lights were on, there were people inside, and I wondered what would happen if I knocked on the door. Would the people inside be as nice as the lonely guy in the woods had been?

I wondered how far from home I was.

"Hey, *you*."

There was a voice, a girl's voice, talking to me from above. Swiveling my head, I looked up, and there was a treehouse there, and looking down from it I was shocked to see Sandy Miller—Sandy Miller from school!

"Hey," I started to say.

"Eeeck!" When I looked up and she saw the robot face, Sandy jumped and shrieked, starting to scream.

"Easy!" I said, waving my arms for her to be quiet. "Don't scream—hold it!"

She did. I guess she suddenly remembered the field trip, because she didn't scream or do anything crazy like that. She froze a minute and stared down at me some more, as if discovering something really amazing (or horrifying) underneath a rock.

"You're that robot!"

"No, I'm . . ." I stopped talking. I couldn't get over seeing her up there. Mostly, I was shocked to see that she had a treehouse. That would have been the second-to-last thing on a list of places where I'd have expected to find Sandy—right before on board a submarine, maybe. "You actually do things outside? I thought you were just the library type."

"What are you talking about?"

"You never play ball or anything at school. No sports."

"Say what?"

"You know what I mean, Sandy."

Sandy actually looked as if she was in awe. "How do you know my name?"

"I sit behind you in science class."

"Huh?"

"It's me, Max."

"Max?"

"Max Helvey? From school? I'm the idea guy."

Sandy shook her head. "No way. I know what you are . . . you're that robot the Abbotts built. Armour, the robot."

I rolled my eyes, and they really did roll; it was a quick roller coaster ride inside my head, as if I'd flipped the TV cameras over fast, and I *immediately* decided never to do that again. "Arthur the robot," I said, recovering.

"What?"

"Its name is Arthur."

"Your name is Arthur?"

"No, like I said, *my* name is Max. This stupid robot that's got my brain, *his* name is Arthur. Remember?"

"I remember. So you're Arthur."

"No, I'm Max. Inside of Arthur. He's stolen my body."

"Excuse me?"

I could hear helicopters circling again, getting closer. *Robot helicopters?* I wondered. *Or the other kind?* "I'm kind of a wanted kid, here," I said. "Can we go into your treehouse? I can explain it all there."

She hesitated, and I didn't blame her, really. Would I have invited some outer space–type machine up to my

43

treehouse for a chat? Not likely; that would have fallen under the category of potential bad things, but I just stared, doing my best to make myself give the robot puppy dog eyes. "Please?" I asked. "I won't hurt you or do anything bad. I'm just in a rotten situation and I don't have anybody friendly to talk to, and . . . well, I'm getting a little scared. Okay?"

Another moment passed, then Sandy nodded. "Sure. Come on up."

So I climbed up and crawled inside. It was a pretty good tree fort, one of the better ones I'd seen, but the wood kind of groaned and creaked when I stepped onto it. "I think you're too heavy," she said.

"For the ladder? The fort?"

"For the tree, I think."

"Maybe."

We waited a minute to see if I was going to fall through the floor of the thing. I didn't, so I looked around some more. It was a cool fort, all right, but Sandy had made it more of a girls' playhouse than something for guys; she actually had curtains over the two windows.

"Aren't you a little old for dolls and stuff?" I asked.

"What do you care?" she asked, retreating into a corner and keeping her back to the wall. "I do what I want to do."

"So did I," I said. "That's how I got into this mess."

"I guess."

I was grateful for the curtains and stuff now, though. If one of those helicopters shined the searchlight at us, they wouldn't be able to see inside as easily.

I told her what had happened. I tried to reason and

found she believed me because I knew so much about her from school; to convince her who I was, I told her a few stories about her from school, including some I'd promised never to repeat, so I won't. She was also looking at me differently and feeling my metal arm, my metal forehead. "You're like something out of a comic book."

Again I was shocked. "You read comic books?"

"Yeah, all the time."

"So do I. Do you read *X-Men?*"

"Yeah, and *Batman.*"

"Wow." I couldn't believe it.

I wondered, though. Was Sandy seeing me as Max from school, or this robot guy?

"So what are you going to do?" she asked.

"I guess the only thing I can do," I said. "Try to find my Mom and Dad. I'll convince them that this is really me somehow, and then we'll make those crazy Abbotts put me back in my body . . . if I can do all this without getting caught and locked up by those crazy Army guys first."

Another helicopter buzzed the yard, shining down its searchlight before flying on, and it was about then that Sandy's father stuck his head out the back door, calling up, "Sandy? Are you all right?"

She stuck her head out the treehouse doorway, calling down to her father, "I'm okay. Why?"

"Just checking. Something strange is going on—you see all those Army helicopters? I wonder if somebody broke out of jail or something?"

"Is there anything on TV?" Sandy wondered.

"What?"

45

"Anything about escaped robots or anything?"

"Very funny," said her father. "Come on down and get ready now, we're just about to leave."

"Just a minute," she called down.

"Where are you going?" I asked this in my best robot whisper.

"To the football game."

My brother's high school football game, I remembered then. *Man, I was gonna miss it. I was missing my body* and *a football game. This sucked.*

Still trying to be nice, Sandy said, "Before I leave, I'll sneak into the house and get a coat or something from my brother's closet."

"I'm not cold. I don't think I get cold."

"Not for the cold, it's so you can hide yourself. Don't you think people are going to notice you with this silver skin and no clothes? You look like a space alien."

"I've heard that one before."

She snuck down from the tree fort and returned a few minutes later with a thick Calpo Vikings football jacket. "Yay, team," I said, slipping it on. "I'm surprised it fits," I told her.

"It should," Sandy said. "My brother's six feet tall and over two hundred pounds."

That's when it happened, the worst bad thing yet, because as we were crawling out of her tree fort, one of the boards on the tree ladder I'd stepped on too heavily ripped free and Sandy slipped, giving out a scream as she fell. I reached to grab her, but I still wasn't used to working the robot's body and missed, and she hit the ground with a sickening *thump*.

46

"Sandy!" I yelled, dropping down fast. She wasn't moving. She was knocked out cold, and I gave her a quick check with my EXTERNAL MEDICAL ANALYSIS.

PATIENT: FEMALE, APPROXIMATE AGE 13
VITAL SIGNS NOMINAL
UNCONSCIOUS—NO APPARENT INJURIES
DIAGNOSIS: STUNNED. RECOVERY IMMINENT.

She was going to be all right, Sandy was, I could tell that right away with this incredible system, but—
"Hey! You! Get away from her!"
"Huh? What?"
I heard another scream, along with the shouting, and saw that Sandy's parents were both charging out the back door, he with a baseball bat and she with a broom handle, as they saw me lumbering over Sandy's unconscious body.
"Get the gun, Jimmy!" The woman was screaming, screaming at the top of her lungs. "Get the shotgun!"
This was not a good thing . . .

— 6 —

MAPLE STREET

I stood there over Sandy, not knowing what to do. What could I do? Sandy's parents, of course, were freaking out, especially her mother. "What is that thing, Jimmy? What is he?"

"I don't know! Get the gun for me!"

The broom-waving woman ran back into the house.

"You get away from my daughter, you monster," said the man, stepping purposely toward me.

"I'm not a monster. I know Sandy from school. I—"

"Move away from her," he growled, charging forward, running into me and shoving, but I was too heavy and too strong. Even with me not resisting, he was unable to move me, but he was crazed, looking up with eyes of fear and anger, and he wasn't going to give up.

I edged back to get out from between the father and his daughter, but I felt horrible about the way he was looking at me; I hadn't done anything. I hadn't done anything, and

48

he was looking at me as if I was some monster, as if I was less than human.

And, of course, I was.

"I didn't do anything to her," I tried to say, but it came out in a whisper; I may have been a robot, but I had feelings. "She fell out of the tree. I'm Max from school, Max Helvey, and this is just a robot body, and I . . ."

He ignored me, putting himself between me and his daughter like a crazed animal defending its cave.

"It's okay," I tried to tell him. "She's going to be okay, she's just stunned, because she slipped coming out of the tree, but my robot brain can tell that she's okay because it's got some biomedical sensors or something, and I . . . I'm not sure . . . but I can tell that she's . . ."

This was crazy. There was absolutely no way anyone was going to believe this story, even if I was standing there in a robot body. Especially with his daughter lying there like that.

I could hear his wife rushing back through the house, crashing through rooms, so I figured it was time to get out of there before I got shot, because I didn't want to test how bulletproof this new body was.

I moved, throwing myself toward some shrubs, but against the shrubs was the redwood fence; but before I remembered this, I crashed through the thing in a loud splinter of wood chips, then I staggered back through to the road and at the same time felt the rage and anger and fear rise from me into a scream.

I, the robot, screamed: *"Ahhhhhhhhhh!"*

The scream came out louder than I could ever have imagined. My robot body shook, the ground trembled; the

49

air itself seemed to vibrate, a distant thunder rumbling a warning to all who could hear. **SENSORY OVERLOAD** warned the computer brain, flashing red and yellow lights in my head.

Who cares? I thought, angry.

I ran, trembling along with the thought: *I can run, but I can't hide . . .*

Running, I found myself on the street now, a real road with houses and street lamps and cars parked along the way. I could also hear police sirens in the distance, though, getting closer, and with thoughts of the Army and robot helicopters pursuing me along with the police, this didn't seem a place to hang around and linger.

So I ran for a while, but eventually slowed to a walk, and why not? The world was my weasel, and I was simmering inside my own mental pot—really angry.

Time out while I explain that crack, which started from a running gag I had a long time ago, where I used to try and work the word "weasel" into every song I sang in school. You know, things like "My Bonnie Lies over the Ocean" becomes "My Weasel Lies over the Ocean," or "She'll Be Coming 'Round the Mountain" becomes "There'll Be Weasels 'Round the Mountain," and every such manner of nonsense.

I wound up near a small neighborhood convenience store, and I approached from the back, trying to stay out of view of traffic, because I saw immediately what I wanted.

I wanted to reach out and touch someone. I very much needed to make a phone call, and there beside the store was a pay phone. I couldn't work the phone out, though;

50

my robot's head was too big to have the receiver by the ear and the mouthpiece anywhere near my mouth.

This is crazy, I thought, and I was just about to rip the wires from the phone headset when I remembered that I could do the whole thing from inside my head; I was a three-million-dollar piece of machinery, so I didn't need a quarter.

Ring. Ring.

My Dad answered. "Hello—?"

"Dad!" I tried to scream. "It's me, Max, I need to—"

Except it wasn't really my dad; it was another machine. There was only the answering machine at home. Of course; they were at the football game. I wondered what the robot impostor in my body thought of the hotdogs he was probably eating—*my* hotdogs.

This wasn't fair. Why was this happening to me?

I decided to try another number, because I'd accessed a telephone number list in the computer's memory, and one of the numbers was the Abbotts'. I decided to let Arthur the robot call home.

This time a real person answered: Dr. Abbott, that crazed Scot himself. "Yes, what is it?" he demanded.

"Greetings from the world of the weasel," I said.

"What?"

"This is your crazed robot speaking. Gimme back my body."

"Laddie? Where are you, laddie?"

"Wouldn't you like to know?" I said. "I want to know where my mom and dad are. I want to talk to them. They'll believe me if I can talk to them."

"You need to come back to the lab."

51

"Why? So you can switch me off?"

"We're not going to switch you off. We're going to help you. You're running out of power, lad; you must know that."

"I know that," I said. I did a quick check of the batteries and then said, "Why won't you people help me?"

"We will help you, lad. We'll check out what you're saying. I suppose anything's possible in this crazy world of science. Perhaps there was more of an accident than we've accounted for."

"Yeah, so is that why you've sicked the Army on me?"

"Uh . . . what?" Abbott sounded wary.

"Yeah, I know about all of that. You and Mrs. Abbott and the Army and evil stealth robot helicopters and who knows what else. You guys said you worked for NASA."

"We once worked for NASA, but as it is—"

"This is supposed to be Calpo, Indiana, Abbott—a normal place if you excuse how it gets around county fair time, and instead, you guys are turning it into some sort of crazy weapons lab."

"There's more to it than that, laddie. Believe me when I say that to you. Please believe me."

And you know what? For a second I almost did.

"We can help you . . ." he started to say, and I started to listen, but that was when something else occurred to me. "Ah, man . . ."

"What is it?"

"You're tracing this call, aren't you? Using the radio signal to figure out exactly where I am?"

"Listen, laddie—"

"You guys are nuts. You don't want to help me. You

52

just want to take me apart and try to figure out if I'm working or if I'm as broken as Pig, or Mouse, or Beast.''

"Listen, boy—''

"That's right,'' I said. "I am a boy.''

Disconnect.

Forget those people.

I made myself scarce for a long while, at least an hour, because I crouched down in some bushes and didn't move at all. What I did was think. After all, if I was supposed to have this supercomputer brain, why not use it to think the problem through before I ran around under swooping helicopters and did something stupid?

The only problem was, every computation came out the same way. The only people in the databank who could really help me were the Abbotts, the very people I wanted to avoid at all costs. I hated the Abbotts. Except they were the only ones who could help me.

The frustration of all of this was making me crazy. I was a robot, and my head was starting to hurt. Walking on, I found myself walking slower than before, and not just to conserve energy. I was feeling depressed, starting to feel a little bit hopeless about my prospects.

This was a bad moment, but it was interrupted by a sudden good thing.

I recognized where I was . . . at the corner of Michelle Road and Detillio Lane. I could see the small DAV building—Daughters of American Veterans—where my mother played bingo sometimes. This was near downtown, and just a few miles or so from home—not even as far as the mall! I could be there in less than an hour, probably.

"What am I waiting for?'' I asked out loud.

53

I started to cross the street and head for home and by doing this made a bad thing happen. I looked both ways, as always, but when I looked left I saw the headlights of a car, so I paused, but the driver watched me instead of the road and swerved at the sight, and *slam!* He collided with the light pole, which fell dramatically, like a tall tree being felled by a lumberjack.

Crash! For me, the moment went in slow motion, but that might have been a defect in the robot's eyes. The pole slammed and crunched down on top of the car's roof, crumpling it in. Electric cables were torn from the pole, sparking and crackling there beside the car door. The three people inside were trapped, but even if they could get out they'd be electrocuted.

INCIDENT! ACCIDENT! alerted my computer brain—the Loser, I remembered now, I was taking all this instruction and advice from the Loser. *POSSIBLE CASUALTIES* flashed the system. *ASSESS AND ASSIST IF POSSIBLE.*

"I need a computer to tell me that?" I said, running over to them. Was I going to electrocute myself, or could I handle this sort of thing?

I didn't know.

People were rushing out of the DAV and their houses to see what the commotion was, and fortunately the street light was out, because otherwise I would have been spotted right away. As it was, I was just another guy in a coat in the dark shadows, so I could get in to help. It was a good thing, because nobody else was going anywhere near those snapping electrical lines.

"Hey! Buddy!" yelled a well-meaning man. "Don't touch those wires or you'll be fried!"

"It's okay," I said, "I've got gloves on."

"Gloves? That won't help a bit, you'll—"

I didn't wait. I grabbed the first cable as if I was grabbing a poisonous snake by the back of the head; I could feel the power surging through the thing like it was evil black water in a garden hose. The robot's computer memory had a few suggestions on how to ground the thing without hurting anyone, so I did. Then I went back to the people in the car.

Nobody was screaming anymore, anyway. "It's going to be okay," I said to them.

I pulled hard on the door and felt the metal bending and warping; the hinge gave way and the door popped off in my hands. "Come on," I said, dropping the door and reaching in to help a lady out. Next came her little son, and finally her husband, who was unconscious, but—as my EXTERNAL MEDICAL SCAN confirmed—not badly hurt.

People were noticing me then, though, even without the light. "It's him," I heard a whisper. "He's that guy, that thing that attacked that girl over on Waylon Avenue; it was on the TV and radio. It *is* him."

"Please . . ." I started to say, but I realized from the looks I was getting that nobody cared about what they'd seen me do. They were pulling their loved ones closer to them and staring at me as if I was the snake, as if I was the black water of electricity surging through those killer cables I'd just grounded. They were looking at me as if I was a monster, and I knew I needed to leave, but some of the bigger men were murmuring together as if they meant to do something about me, so I pulled myself up to my tallest height and gave out my *SENSORY OVERLOAD* of a vicious roar.

They wanted a monster? I could be a monster: *"Arrrrrggggh!"*

The screaming crowd scattered.

I walked on . . .

7

THE BIG GAME

Fine, I thought, defensive and hurt and angry. I even roared it out loud: "If they won't let me help, if they think I'm a monster, then I'll *be* a monster." *Maybe I am a monster at heart. Maybe we all are—after all, the Abbotts didn't seem so far off. Who cares?* I asked that question right out loud: "Who cares?"

Nobody was listening to my yelling, though; I was walking a nearly deserted street and might have been scared if I hadn't been so busy scaring everyone else. When a head popped out of a door to see what rough beast was slouching down the street, it quickly disappeared inside after my roar.

This was nutty . . .

I wanted to head toward home, but that was the side of town where the swooping helicopters seemed to be concentrating, so I took my time and wandered in that direction by way of downtown.

Downtown Calpo was a place I'd never spent much time. A dying city, the area consisted of a lot of closed and closing businesses which loomed like dark cathedrals of shadow; I slumped through these shadows, avoiding the corner lights and wondering why. This was a time I *should* be angry, I knew; so much fear and torment and pain was being tossed at me, so why not go crazy?

Really—and this was a serious question—why not ball my silver fists and crash through the soon-to-be-boarded-up plate glass windows of Webber's Bike Shoppe and steal a fancy ten-speed? There were two-thousand-dollar bikes in there, I knew. Terrific road cruisers, bikes a person could race away into the neverlands, and start life over as a superhero in an indestructible body, except . . .

Except I was no thief. Even if I was a robot.

All things considered, I just wanted to find some help and go home. But thirty-six hours was my deadline.

Thirty-six hours before my new life ended.

What was I going to do until then?

"Hey, you!" yelled a voice.

"Freeze!" said another.

Stopped in front of the bike store, I turned toward the sound; there, standing before a parked patrol car, were two Calpo police officers, one of whom had his gun out. He must have been the more scared one, because he held the pistol in both hands and they were shaking.

"Don't you move," he shouted. "Don't you move!"

What were they going to do, shoot me? And if they did, what happened then?

I stepped toward them, just meaning to talk. "Listen to me, guys, you don't understand what's happening here."

58

"Stop!"

"I should be the one calling the police; I'm the one who's been robbed. You can help me."

"I'm warning you! Freeze!"

"Some maniac's stolen my body—"

Blam! Blam! The cop with the shaking hands fired twice, but the bullets bounced off my metal body, one of them off my head. It ricocheted against the concrete with a *ping-ping* squeal and then there was a loud *pop!* One of the front tires of the police car had been pierced by their own bullet and gone flat.

"Stop shooting at me," I yelled, immediately feeling stupid because I said it like I was yelling, *"Stop throwing snowballs at me."*

Except they weren't snowballs and the cop took another two shots. The bullets ricocheted off me as well. Then he took off running, but not before taking a final shot, and this one surprised me by not bouncing off—it slammed into me.

Zing! I stumbled from the impact of this one, and electric static flashed before my right eye, the internal balance of the robot body going out of kilter for just a moment before I brought myself upright and took another step. The shooting cop was gone, leaving his partner standing there alone, pointing only his finger. "You're uh . . . uh . . . you're under arrest," he stammered.

"Arrrrrghhhh!" I said, raising my hands over my head like claws and giving a roar. That did it; the second cop ran, too, both of them abandoning their damaged police car.

Well, I had my wish now; *I'm a monster,* I thought.

59

They've made me a monster, they've turned me into this thing and I know that inside the machine it's just me, but they don't even know what me is; and now I've got police shooting at me!

Not to mention that I was shot—*for-real shot*—and that was affecting the way I was moving, the way this stupid robot body was working. Again static flashed in front of my right eye, and I wasn't sure if the machine wouldn't just fall apart in the next few seconds.

Then they would win, all those people who had done this to me.

Time was running out. I may not have been a superhero, but I was bright enough to figure that one out. **AMES FIELD,** the computer side of my brain was flashing.

Huh?

PARENTS AND SIBLING—PROBABLE LOCATION BASED ON PREVIOUS DATA ANALYSIS.

What? Then I realized my computer brain was reminding me where Mom and Dad were, and where I should be going. Now.

Ames Field.

Of course. I wasn't that far away. I needed to get to the football game to find my mom and dad and brother—and, I knew, *myself,* and I needed to get there now . . .

Ames Field stood tall against my sight, the extra-high stadium lights shining down on the walls and the field within. This was the place where the high school and junior high school played all their football and soccer games. My brother Mike was in there somewhere, I knew, along with my parents and—*ugh*—me.

My *body,* anyway. Again I had the shuddering realization: that *thing* in there had *my* body, and I was going to swipe it back from the thing that had stolen it from me.

Occasional roars erupted from the crowd, meaning one side or the other had done something interesting. *Get me out on the field,* I thought. The old Max would have been stepped on, stepped across, and tossed aside, but this new body would be hard to stop on a football field.

There was an interesting image. *First and ten, from the thirteen-yard line, with the Calpo Vikings down by five points as I lined up at running back with my superhero body. The ball is snapped to quarterback Mike Helvey, who hands it off to his brother Max, the idea guy, just before getting himself slammed facedown in the mud. Despite the heavy rains, running back Max has no trouble with his traction. He seems a creature possessed, unstoppable, as he crushes through the defenders toward the goal line. Yes! Max Helvey scores another touchdown! This guy has what it takes, this guy is going to go all the way, this guy—*

This guy isn't even human.

I want my body back—*now*.

So I went to the football game to find my parents. But what was I supposed to do? Walk straight into the stadium and start looking around for my mom and dad?

Nothing better came to mind.

The first person I approached was the old man taking tickets at the gate; I recognized him as Mr. Winters, one of the English teachers from school, doing his part in the name of school spirit. Half asleep, as always, he merely

61

grunted as I walked right up to him. "Ticket, please," he said, not even looking up.

"I don't have a ticket," I answered.

"Then it's two dollars and fifty cents to get inside. Money goes to support the team colors."

"Team colors? What are you talking about?"

He looked up then and went a pale white upon seeing me. "Oh, my . . ."

"Don't start screaming," I said, stepping forward. "I'm not up for it."

He wasn't listening. "Oh, my . . ."

"Can I go in?"

"Go! Go!"

I went into the stadium and up the ramp. Almost immediately I ran into people looking for hot dogs and soft drinks, and, well, I think it's safe to say that that's when the first screaming and shouting began.

One of the kids I knew, though; Benjamin Brooks, from my English class—and I grabbed him by the arm before he could run off with the others. "Hang on, Ben, hold it," I said.

"Ow!" he said, yelling from the way I pinched his arm.

"I need to talk to you."

"Ow! Let me go! What are you?"

"It's me, Max. I—"

"Help! Help!" Ben was screaming, and I could see nothing but absolute terror. "Don't hurt me," he said, trembling, and stumbled in my grasp.

"Why would I hurt you?"

Rip! Ben's shirt tore and he scrambled away, leaving me standing there with tatters of cloth in my hand, again looking like the big and vicious beast.

Which makes you wonder what I was thinking about, even going to the stadium, but we're not talking about normal thinking occurring here. We're talking about end-of-the-world–type thinking, and I didn't care anymore. All I wanted to do was find my mom and dad.

I gritted my brand new solid-steel teeth and walked on. Climbing the ramp, I came out into overhead lights and the roar of a crowd. *Forget the San Diego Chicken, ladies and gentlemen, how about some applause for the Calpo Viking Robot?* That was just in my head, though. Using my sharp new electronic eyes, I scanned the crowd for my parents—

—RANGEFINDER, ELECTRONIC TRACKING—

My mother. My father.

The scoreboard said "CALPO 21   MERYLVILLE 17," with a few minutes left before halftime, but I could feel attention shifting from the game to me. I tried to search faster, before the real trouble started.

I knew who I was looking for; all the computer inside my head had to do was do the rest.

The crowd was noticing me now, though, and an excited babble started, followed by shrieks. There were almost a thousand people at the game, and most of them were on their feet by now, trying to make tracks, trying to get away from whatever I was.

SELECTIVE DISSEMINATION—
DISCRIMINATE AND SEEK—

The game was over now, with even the football players and coaches and referees running for cover. Why? What had I done? *Besides break out of a lab, attack a kid, cause a car accident, fight with some cops, and flatten their tires?*

"Ah, man . . ." I said aloud. My computer was rattling through images of the people, trying to find Mom and Dad or Mike, but for all I knew, they weren't even there.

Except—

I thought I saw my mother then, and I felt a rush of excitement and tried to get her attention, waving at her, although she was reacting with all the rest of them.

"Mom!" I yelled. "Mom! Dad!"

They saw me—everybody saw me—and I saw myself, that slimy little thug-robot-kid hiding in my body, and he looked more scared than anyone. *He—it—me,* standing there with my mom and dad, screaming and shouting that the monster was coming.

"Mom! Wait!"

She wasn't waiting; none of them were. Maybe it wasn't even her—it was difficult to tell with everyone fleeing. They were off with the stampede away from me, the crowd of people charging toward the exits to escape from the all-consuming terror . . . of me.

"Wait!" I couldn't help but scream this out, but there really wasn't any point to it. I was standing alone in the midst of an empty football field, in the midst of an almost empty stadium, watching the world run away from me as fast as it could . . .

| 8 |

SHOWTIME

There's a scene in an old Frankenstein movie where the angry townspeople burn down this old church with the monster trapped inside. Nobody feels sorry for the thing or tries to find out what his real problem is. They just run along and do it. So when the noise of sirens headed toward the stadium began to overtake the sounds of people running away from Ames Field, I figured the real trouble was about to start. *Time to get out of here.*

I slinked back down the ramp, meaning to head out the way I'd come, but it led toward the parking lot, where I ran right into a bunch of people standing there with fire extinguishers and a big hose. *The last stand of the volunteer fire department,* I thought, except all of a sudden they turned it all on me with a furious *whoosh!*

That set off alarms inside my computer brain, buzzes and flashes of lots of colors and warnings that told me this: I was not quite as waterproof as the Abbotts might

65

have wanted their robot to be. The bullet from when the cop had shot me had pinged around inside, ripped through some wires and metal, and produced some leaks, and small parts of me were short-circuiting.

WARNING—SYSTEM FAILURE WARNING
WARNING—GENERAL ALARM
WARNING—

Wonderful, I thought. *I'm a toaster in the bathtub.*

I turned back. As I did, I could see now that many of the people had run only as far as the parking lot, and those who weren't in their cars trying to leave were clustered in groups, apparently trying to decide what to do about me. Several dozen flashlights flickered, aimed in my direction, and a few voices shouted out with, "There he is— they've got him now. What's he doing?"

Plan B had better be good, I thought, shuffling back through the hall, splashing and dripping water and fire extinguisher foam up the ramp to the railing that stood a few feet above the field. I couldn't crawl over it, especially as slippery and wet as I was, but I could rip the actual metal of the rail in half as if it was paper and drop myself down to the green with a *thump.*

The other side of Ames Field was strictly bleachers and chain-link fence, so escaping that was going to be a whole lot easier. From there I'd head to my own house to hide until I could figure out what to do next.

There was no real reason to go there, I knew; Mom and Dad were not going to be in my corner, what with the way they'd run along with the others, but there was something whimpering inside of me . . . something quiet that just wanted someplace familiar to be, a safe place to hide.

I started stepping across the field, over the fifty-yard line, noticing dropped helmets—and the football. Another thing I was going to be in trouble for: Calpo would probably have to forfeit the game—*called on account of crazed robot attack.* Everybody was going to hate me, I was thinking, but other than that, I was barely paying attention to anything around me, so it was no surprise that in a sudden instant I found myself bathed in bright white light from above, and when I looked up I squinted at first, wondering if on top of everything else I was going to be kidnapped by aliens from space, but no . . .

Not quite.

My electronic brain automatically shuffled through the different eyes available to me and that dimmed the glow; it was now as if I was wearing dark sunglasses, and I saw that the helicopter above me was different, with three sets of smaller rotor blades, but as they chopped the air, they could barely be heard.

It was a ghost chopper, nearly invisible and silent, unheard except by me, now that I realized it was there.

A stealth helicopter?

Nowhere to run, either. So I stood there a long moment in the light, expecting a loudspeaker voice to begin screaming at me from above, but that didn't happen. Instead, there was a radio crackle inside my head, and **TELE-COMMUNICATIONS CONTACT—RADIO ADDRESS— ACCESS?** flickered as if a phone was ringing.

So I answered. "I need help," I said.

"Cease all activity and stand yourself down for recapture," said the voice, and the voice didn't sound any more human than I did. It was a strange, squelchy sort of electronic scrambled tinny thing, like the fake voices used for computers.

"Who *is* this?" I asked.

"Cease all activity and stand yourself down for recapture," repeated the voice.

"Are you a person or a machine?"

No reply.

"The least you can do is say who you are," I said to the helicopter floating a hundred feet above me. Then the computer side of my brain asked the same question, but in its own way. It transmitted, *IDENT FOF—FRIEND OR FOE? CODE 72771.*

Against its will, I presume, the helicopter immediately chattered back, *IDENT FOF CODE 72771/WINGMAN 3301/UNMANNED.*

Wingman, unmanned. That was definitely the stealth chopper they'd been talking about before. Now that I knew what I was looking for, my computer brain accessed its data and determined that Wingman was a series of experimental unmanned attack helicopters the Army was working on, and this was one of them. There was no one on the silent stealth helicopter. Still, it repeated its message: *"Cease all activity."*

"Or what?"

"If you attempt flight, you will be terminated."

"Flight? What are you talking about? I can't fly."

"If you attempt to avoid recapture, you will be terminated."

"What do you mean, 'terminated'?"

"I am equipped with laser-guided armor-piercing high-explosive shells."

"Say what? You're going to shoot me?"

"You will be terminated."

Terrific. They had brought the big robot boys in after me, and they were willing to rip up the high school football field with exploding rocket bullets to do it.

"Come on, guy," I said, standing there in the light at the fifty-yard line, trying to appeal to it with something we had in common. "We're both the same. We're both machines they've built to do the nasty things they don't have the guts to do themselves. They want to shoot me into space and they want to send you off to war—who cares if we get blown up?"

"Cease all activity or you will be terminated. Stand down for recapture."

"You know, I've got a cat at home that listens better than you do."

"Stand down."

I played this for all it was worth, pretending to be a machine just like it was. "Okay, so what? You're on their side instead of mine? Doesn't that make you a traitor? We should be together on this thing."

"Stand by for transmission," said the helicopter. *"Relaying—"* Static, then I heard crazy Abbott's voice. *"Arthur? Are yae there, boy?"*

"This is Max."

"Thank God you've not done anything too terrible."

"Why would I do anything terrible? *You* guys are the bad guys," I said.

69

"We're on the way to get you. We can make everything better. We can make everything okay."

"Okay? Yeah, right, Abbott. You're going to take me apart piece by piece and try to figure out what went wrong with your precious little machine."

"I won't let them do that, laddie."

"I'm headed for the same basement junkyard that Pig and Mouse and Beast wound up in. And my buddy here, the talking helicopter, is going to help you do it."

"Easy, laddie—"

So I pulled out all the stops. I stopped using my voice and switched quickly to the computer side, trying to lay in some common ground with the hovering monster above me; I remembered seeing this in a movie once, about a computer that took over the world.

I transmitted the following to the helicopter's computer brain:

$$1 \times 1 = 1$$
$$1 \times 2 = 2$$
$$1 \times 3 = 3 \ldots$$

I started doing math, times tables, for the stupid thing. And the computer inside my head worked fast. In less than thirty seconds it was up to $12 \times 12 = 144$, and in less than a minute after that it was zapping algebra, geometry, trig, calculus, and lots of other things the human side of my brain didn't understand at all. I—*we*—were laying it on thick and heavy, trying to establish a relationship with my helicopter guard.

70

Common ground. Best way to establish a relationship, right? Figure out if we both like *X-Men* comic books, and then talk about them for a while. Same way I got to be friends with Cory.

Come on, come on, I thought, as we zoomed through mathematics and into advanced physics, things guys like Einstein and the Abbotts would have loved. Still no reply from the helicopter, although I knew if I took three steps the thing would blast me into the next world.

(If there is *a next world,* I thought, *and if the next world for robots isn't a heaven populated by old calculators, retired sewing machines, and junk cars. Hmmm . . .)*

Come on, come on, I thought, standing there and wondering how many minutes it would be before the other helicopters arrived . . . the ones with the Abbotts and the other guys sent in to capture me and rip me apart.

Come on, I kept sending and sending . . .

"Stand by for reply transmission," said the helicopter.

This is it, I thought. Another stand-down order, and probably the announcement that the bad guys were arriving on scene with their pliers, blowtorches, and scrap buckets.

"Stand by . . ." said the helicopter above me. Then it totally surprised, totally shocked me by answering back with the following:

$$1 \times 1 = 1$$
$$1 \times 2 = 2$$
$$1 \times 3 = 3 \ldots$$

A minute later it had zipped through the same math and

calculus I had; seconds after that, I felt something change in the calculations and formulas. Seconds after that, I realized that not only the computer side of my brain, but a part of the real human side, part of my *human* personality, was being passed along to this U.S. Army superweapon.

How much? I wondered. *How much is going across? Enough?*

A few seconds after that the helicopter spoke, sounding confused. *"Transmission of data was assumed to be encrypted . . ."*

"Yeah?"

"Wingman assumptions presumed . . . I mean, I thought your message was in code."

"Yeah?"

"You were not talking in code. You were talking to me with your mind. You . . . you shared your mind. With me."

"Yeah."

"Why would you share your mind? I am merely an instrument of military superiority. The complications of your mind surprise me. You . . ."

I waited: this was important.

"You are not just a robot."

"No," I agreed.

A few long, scary seconds passed, and then the helicopter above me said, in its computer voice, *"Good luck, my friend. I . . . I . . ."*

"You what?"

Sounding even more surprised, the helicopter said, *"I . . . I think, therefore I am."*

That was profound, so I said, "Yes, you are."

"Thank you," it said after a moment, and with that

72

it let me go, flying away on its own, like a great bird soaring off.

The Army boys are going to love me for that, I thought. A robot helicopter with a new—but not necessarily *improved*—personality, patrolling the night sky as I disappeared from the football field as fast as I could . . .

9

HOME

At the beginning of every comic book you usually have the same scene, where the hero has just nearly been blown up or killed, but by quick work of his wits, has managed to escape. He's tired but feels good because he made it.

I knew that feeling, because now, once again, *I* had made it.

I was getting almost good at this. I had faced destruction and prevailed. *Yay, robot man!*

There was a downside. I was starting to actually feel tired now—a kind of mechanical sort of ache, like the noise a squeaky door makes. I was also suffering from the occasional electronic flash that sparked in my right eye whenever my foot came down too hard. This seemed to be a side effect of having been shot and sprayed with water and fire extinguisher foam.

So much for being indestructible.

Somehow, I managed to slip out of the back of Ames

Field and get home without being blasted or captured or shot. When I arrived there, though, creeping quietly up the side street, Mom and Dad and Mike weren't home.

Naturally.

Just the family dog and cat.

The front door was locked, but I was so anxious to get inside I twisted it anyway and was surprised when the thing broke off clean in my hand. So much for a nice, quiet entrance. I gave the door a hard push and heard the lock shatter, and the door pushed open.

"Mom! Dad!" I screamed.

No answer, except I could hear Vin, our dog, a German shepherd, snarling a few feet across the room. He didn't recognize me and growled and snapped as if he was going to lunge for my throat at any second.

I didn't want him to do that—he might have hurt his teeth. Like in the old joke—what would a car-chasing dog ever do if he actually caught one?

"Vin, hey, it's me," I said.

No way. The dog did not believe me and didn't recognize my voice because it wasn't my voice, just that of the machine. I took an easy, careful step toward him, but Vin suddenly whimpered, jerking away and running down the hall to the kitchen and out the dog door.

"Oh, man . . ." I said, wandering slowly into the living room, home at last but still trying to find out what to do. I tramped up the stairs to my room, but it was strange. I sat down on the bed, but it creaked loudly and sagged beneath my weight before the boards beneath the box springs gave out completely.

Ka-thump! Me and the bed hit the floor.

75

Way too big. I was way too big.

What was I going to do, creep around my own house like Goldilocks from the three bears story? Keep testing the bed frames until finding one which was *just right?*

No way.

I grabbed a stack of comics, thinking I could just read while I waited for Mom and Dad to get home—that was going to be a scene—but as I did, something short-circuited in my electronic brain and my hand squeezed too hard, scrunching the papers with a sudden reflex and ripping a *Spiderman* cover.

"Ah, man," I said, looking at my robot hand as if it was something not even connected to my body, and I remembered just then that it wasn't. It wasn't connected to my body; none of this was; and I dropped the comics and walked over to the bathroom.

The mirror. I looked at myself in the mirror.

A silver aluminum-foil-colored face with robot eyes stared back at me. "Why is this happening?" I asked.

The robot in the mirror didn't answer.

Maybe it isn't, I thought. *Maybe this was all some sort of crazy dream that I'm going to wake up from anytime now.*

Anytime now.

I looked out in the hall and saw Sherman standing there, then. "Sherman," I said. "Hey, Sherman . . ."

The cat just stared at me, puzzled, his eyes squinting, looking very orange. It wasn't as if the cat was totally rejecting me, like my dog had; Sherman was thinking things through, doing math in his head, the way he always

76

seemed to when he bumped into a problem like a closed door, or something he was curious about.

Sherman the cat was trying to make up his mind about me, what or who I was, and he was having a difficult time of it.

"Come on, guy," I said. "It's me."

Decision made. He didn't believe it. Sherman bolted down the stairs after Vin.

Sirens now; I could definitely hear the police coming, and it didn't take a supercomputer brain to know who they were coming after. Inside my head I found I could tune into the police radio frequencies and hear that they were being told: *"Surround the house. Don't let that thing escape, but do not try to apprehend. Wait for the soldiers and the scientists to arrive on scene so they can organize the capture."*

Here we go, I thought. It was a scene right out of one of those old monster movies they ran on Saturday afternoons. The police and the Army were going to surround this place and start attacking, and I was going to fight for a while, but eventually they would destroy me—and half the town—and then the head scientist would get the girl and everybody would live happily ever after as the movie said "The End" . . .

This seemed to fall into the category of bad things, I thought.

I went back to my room, past my broken bed, and peeked out the window.

Below me, the outside of the house was bathed in so much light that it seemed like daytime, and helicopters were buzzing the place at what sounded like rooftop level.

77

I peeked out the curtains and saw two green Army trucks across the street, parked on the neighbors' lawn as dozens of uniformed soldiers leaped out the back, all carrying rifles.

That was all I saw before backing away. Peeking out the window didn't seem like a good thing.

I felt scared, but alert and sharp. My breathing wasn't affected and my heart wasn't pounding because I wasn't breathing and didn't have a heart. So I just wondered what to do next.

Why not just wait? I wondered. *What are they going to do? Shoot their way in here? No way . . .*

Then again, those Army guys probably weren't going to wait forever.

But I was a monster, wasn't I? I felt like fighting. I felt like raging.

Who was I kidding? I felt like hiding underneath my bed.

Where were Mom and Dad?

INCOMING MESSAGE flashed on my telecommunications channel, but at the same time, a voice on a loudspeaker called out: *"Attention to the thing in the house . . ."*

"That would be me," I said out loud, lumbering downstairs and over to the living-room window. I broke the glass with my fist—how many times would a guy get away with doing that in his own house?—and roared outside, "Attention to the *things* in the street . . ."

They waited a moment. So did I, and then I said, "Can I help you guys?"

"That's not funny, robot."

"Not very," I agreed. "So what happens next?"

"Give it up."

"Give *what* up? I'm not *doing* anything."

That shut them up for a few seconds, but only a few. The voice said, *"You are a public menace."*

"You could have a point there," I said, recalling everything that had happened so far. "I feel like a menace. So how about if I come out there and start ripping your Army guys apart? I could eat a tank for breakfast," I said. "Maybe I'll start by throwing a truck at you."

"We have rockets and shells that would make mincemeat of you, robot. There wouldn't be enough left of you to set off an airport metal detector. So go ahead and make my day."

"Okay," I said after a moment's thought. "I've got a solution."

"And what would that be?"

"Gimme back my body."

"Come out and we'll talk about it."

"Yeah, right."

But I still had no options. My dog and cat, long gone, offered no opinions. Escape seemed impossible.

So I surrendered.

"Okay, coppers. You got me. I'm coming out!" I said.

I walked out the front door and it was as if I was the head alien coming down out of the flying saucer, because I was completely surrounded by dozens of men, all looking terrified, all pointing their guns and rifles at me. "Take me to your leader!" I actually said, but nobody laughed.

Several of the guys appeared to be Army commandos, and I guess they were, because they didn't act scared, like the others. Three guys ran over to take charge of me. "Don't move."

"I'm not moving."

"Watch out."

"I'm watching."

The biggest commando snarled as he clamped something on the back of my neck—a metal computerized something which made my body go rigid, as if I'd stuck a fork into a light socket. "Ow!"

"This'll freeze you."

That it did. My mind still worked, but I was unable to control my robot body—I was disconnected from it, and that was a scary, helpless feeling.

"Enforcement clamp," he said to me. "You won't be moving now unless we say it's okay." Then he added, very smugly, "Consider this lesson number one, buddy. No machine will ever beat a man . . ."

10

PROJECT PROMETHEUS

They put me in an Army slammer.

I was carried and lifted up into the back of one of the Army trucks and guarded by soldiers, which seemed pointless, since the clamp on the back of my metal neck made it impossible for me to move. The truck bumped and rocked through the night . . . how long and how far, I wasn't sure, but it couldn't have been for more than a couple of hours, which made for an interesting discovery.

The discovery that the Army had a big secret base that close to Calpo.

The ride wasn't so nice because the Army guys guarding me were rude, mocking and making fun of me. "I could use something like you at home," one of them said. "Mow my lawn and do my taxes at the same time."

"Yeah," said another. "Maybe it could mind-meld with the microwave and figure out why my popcorn always burns."

81

"Hey, if you could help program my VCR, maybe I'll get you an oil change at Jiffy-Lube."

On and on it went. Why not? I wasn't human to them, and that's human nature: torment the strange.

Now, I've never been one of those conspiracy guys, believing in ghosts, UFOs, aliens, the Loch Ness monster, and all that stuff the government supposedly knows about but keeps secret. But if the government had secret bases and robot helicopters—*and robot kids now*—what else did they have?

The truck was driven into some basement facility and they loaded me onto a hospital gurney and rolled me down some halls and into a locked room, where they left me waiting for a long while.

I didn't sleep—that was something I was realizing. Although the computer brain allowed for something called **ENERGY CONSERVATION MODE,** where I lay motionless, parked in the corner of the tiny room I was being held in, my mind was sharp and alert all through the wait, until finally an Army officer in a camouflage uniform with two side-by-side silver bars on his collar let himself in to talk to me.

Bzzzz. The door clicked open and he entered, taking a general look at the situation and then a general look at me.

At first he just stared. Then he said, "Well, I will say something: you are definitely like a box of breakfast cereal."

"Huh?"

"New and improved." He smirked at his own joke. "I worked on the Pig and Mouse projects, and I'd finally

82

given up Mr. and Mrs. Abbott as complete losers. Then came the capital 'L' Loser, I guess. I'm surprised."

"I may be the new-and-improved breakfast cereal," I said. "But you guys are the real flakes."

"Nice one," he nodded. "So, notice anything about this room . . . or the door?"

"Just a door question?" I said. "No names, no introductions, just a door question?"

"Do—you—notice—*anything?*" He snapped it out word by word, a question—an order.

"The door," I said. "Sure." I'd noticed it from the first moment I was brought inside.

"Ah . . ."

"It's glowing."

"You see the aura. That's fascinating. It's on a light frequency that humans can't see, did you know that? Only robots with electronic eyes."

"I didn't know that."

"Haven't you tried to push your way out?"

"No."

"Well, go ahead and try."

"I'm clamped and can't move."

"Oh, that's right," he said, smiling as if the joke had been on me again, and then he came over and removed the clamp. "Now, please rise and try the door."

What's the point of that? I wondered. "I'd rather not," I said. "I'm not a pet doing tricks."

"Pity. But you'd never succeed anyway, because you want to know what that glowing light you see means?"

"Sure."

83

"It's there because the door, the walls, everything about this room, in fact, are magnetically reinforced."

"Huh?"

"I presumed with your Loser brain you'd—"

"Look, my name's Max. I'm just a kid, and you're talking way over my head."

"Uh-huh. Max." He spoke like he was humoring me and wanted me to *know* he was humoring me. "Well, *Max,* it's a special new technology—invisible waves of energy that reinforce the link between the molecules. Superman couldn't break out of here. And let me tell you this, robot. I read *Superman* when I was a kid; I know all about Superman. I always considered him a friend of mine. And you, robot, are no Superman."

"I know Superman," I said. "I know the X-Men, too, and Superman's a wimp."

"Funny," he said, but the guy seemed offended. "I am Captain Sellers," he said. "United States Army Special Projects, Research and Development Alpha Division. Officer of security."

"Sounds like the guy at the mall who chases shoplifters."

"Uh-huh." He stared at me for a good long moment. "My, you are a glorious disaster," he finally said.

"Huh?"

"Have no regrets," he said. "You are the prototype. For generations to come—maybe forever—scientists and even ordinary people will remember that you were the first. The breakthrough robot."

"What are you talking about?"

"That newfangled brain of yours, the way it works so

much better than anyone ever dreamed. The adaptability of the body to the loser.''

"I am not a loser.''

"Yes, you are.'' Again he smiled.

"Okay,'' I said. "So what about me?''

"Well . . . we need to have another serious look at your components.''

"My components?''

"I need to know what exactly is making you tick like this.''

"Making me tick?''

"Okay,'' he said. "We're going to rip you apart. Satisfied?''

He was in the cell with me, and I stepped forward. "So why don't I just rip you apart first? Huh?''

"I don't know. Why *don't* you?''

I glared at him. Well, "glare'' is a tough description, because the face of the robot body I was trapped inside had a lot of expressions to choose from, but who could figure them all out? Some of the things on the list were:

SMILE   *[specify selection—chuckle, grin, bemused, cheery, surprised but happy, delighted, amused, angry but cynically amused {note submenus}]*

FROWN   *[specify selection—groan, frump, growl, grimace . . .*

The list went on for a while, allowing for the optional

facial expressions I could go with, but it was too confusing so I just went with *GAZE WITH CONTEMPT—STAT.*

"I'm not like you guys," I said.

"No? Why is that?"

"I won't hurt you just because I don't understand you."

That stumped him for a minute, but then he said, "Ah, so you're choosing to be superior."

"Yeah. That's me. Captain Superior, like in a comic."

"But you claim to be human. Only human."

"I was. Maybe I'm a little bit better than that now."

"That's a dangerous thought, Mr. Robot."

The door buzzed again and opened, and this time it was the Abbotts. They both bounced in and Mr. Abbott was especially excited—he'd even shaved and pulled back his long red hair into a ponytail. "Arthur, laddie, have you been damaged?"

I gave him a long look before answering. "Not yet, but the Army guys say that's the plan."

"What?" Abbott looked confused.

"I guess there's no choice, really," said Mrs. Abbott.

What do you mean?" asked the crazy redheaded Scot, turning on his wife.

"It's out of our hands," she said.

"He's back with us now—"

"No," said the captain. "Your wife has signaled the project back over to the Army."

That shocked Abbott, and he turned to his wife. "What right did you have to do that?"

"Every right. I'm a cocreator on the project, every bit as responsible as you are."

86

"Surely, but why bow to the Army? They're every bit as bad as NASA."

Mrs. Abbott looked at me when she said, "This isn't a Pig or a Beast. This thing is dangerous. Could be dangerous."

"He's not dangerous," said Abbott, and he whispered urgently to me, "Tell them you're not dangerous, laddie."

"I'm not dangerous."

"There, he's said it for himself. And we've programmed him never to lie."

They had?

"The time for decision is past, anyway," reminded Captain Sellers. "He's quite an accomplishment, but there's been too much brouhaha already."

Brouhaha?

Ha . . . ha . . . ha . . .

"I feel for you, Dr. Abbott," said Captain Sellers. "But we can't dispatch helicopters and soldiers and just let you go back to business as usual. We do have the taxpayers to consider. They paid for the thing, after all. He's government property."

"I'm government property?" I asked.

"Just like a mailbox."

Mrs. Abbott's tone of voice showed she had been complaining about me a lot, saying that "This entire experiment has been set for failure from the first moment. The first moment."

"No, no, it has not," Abbott answered back. "Don't you understand?"

"Well, now that the project is terminated, I'll handle the disposition," said Captain Sellers.

"I've not yet terminated the project," said Abbott.

"I have," answered Sellers. "Security is gone, the entire town has seen this thing—"

"Arthur—"

"They've all seen Arthur, and it's time to move him to a more secure environment where he can be properly studied."

"You can't do this."

"Look, let's not discuss this here," said the captain. "I think we're, uh, upsetting your creation. Let's go to my office."

So they left me then, but as they did, I saw Abbott do a curious thing. He hesitated a moment so he would be the last one to leave the room, and as he did, he tapped the magnetic locking pad on the outside of the door before he closed it.

Then he gave me a wink.

A wink? At first I thought crazy old Abbott was having a breakdown, starting with an eye twitch, but at that moment I saw the aura around the door change colors. It was something only I could see, but I knew right away what Abbott had done.

He'd unlocked the door for me . . .

II

THE LAB

There's a *GhoulMan* comic where our hero—a once mild-mannered librarian who has learned the secrets of near immortality—is captured by the evil Venezuela, his arch-enemy. GhoulMan had attacked Venezuela's fortress to rescue the captured scientist Ralph (okay, so Ralph wasn't the best name for a scientist). GhoulMan freed Ralph but was captured when he returned to destroy the Blue Laser device.

(Sorry . . . I love this stuff . . . I love comics . . .)

Anyway . . . locked away deep in a dungeon, GhoulMan is helped—*he thinks*—by Venezuela's shifty sidekick Cassandra, who "accidentally" drops the sonic key to the dungeon's lock. GhoulMan uses the sonic key to make his escape, then rushes to where he has hidden Ralph the scientist—only to discover his escape has been set up just to help Venezuela recapture them both.

It was a trap. Which got me thinking . . .

Was this a trick?

What could they possibly want to trick me into? I wasn't hiding any scientists. I wasn't a real superhero. I was just a scared kid trapped in a robot's body.

Then something occurred to me. Maybe Abbott had finally realized that.

Maybe he was starting to feel a little guilty about what he had done, wiring me into that computer stuff. I wasn't exactly ready to start trusting Abbott quite yet—another thought had occurred to me, and for all I knew, this was some sort of test they were running. After all, if Pig was programmed to go through walls, then maybe I was, too. Maybe this was all for someone's amusement.

But I was a person, not a robot. Perhaps Abbott was a decent enough guy and had finally realized that. And if I waited around long enough, then something along the lines of a serious bad thing was going to happen.

I watched the door.

What are you waiting for? What are you waiting for?

The thought repeated through my head like a computer loop, a statement clicking again and again, and saw as I did a sudden vision of my ending. *The door opened and Captain Sellers returned, accompanied by two very stern-looking technicians who reapplied the clamp to the back of my neck, lifted me onto a cart, and wheeled me down the hall.*

I could still talk and tried to get them to answer back by saying, "Come on, what's going on? Where's Abbott? Where's Mrs. Abbott?"

"Don't worry about it, robot."

"I'm worried about it," I said. "What's the deal? Come

90

on? Why do you guys hate me? Just because I'm different? Because I'm silver and don't look the same as you guys do?"

"No," said Captain Sellers, very seriously. "I hate you because I don't understand you. I don't know what you really are, or how you got here, or what you might do."

"So does that give you the right to destroy me?"

No answer from Sellers or his pals. They wheeled me into a very clean, brightly lit room where soldiers in white smocks gathered quickly around me, each bearing a tool, or a cutting saw, or screwdrivers and pliers, and the computer in my head flashed DANGER! DANGER! MASTER ALARM! SYSTEM COLLAPSE! as those guys whirred and buzzed and ripped me apart and—

Why was I doing all this thinking? Was I computer crazy?

Get out of here!

I waited a long while, longer than I should have, all the while wondering if Captain Sellers or any of the other Army guys would realize what Abbott had done, but nobody reappeared to restart the magnetic lock and I stared at the door, which was no longer glowing.

Okay, I thought. Even if I escape from the lab, escape from the Army base, where am I going? My power supply was running down. Who was I going to find in that amount of time who would—or could—possibly help me get my body back?

The answer was obvious: Abbott himself. Clearly he was worried about what he'd done, even if he wasn't quite positive what that might be. He'd left the magnetic lock

91

off so that I could get away—obviously he meant for me to come to him.

Dr. Frankenstein is calling the creature home, I thought. He was calling the monster back before the townspeople ripped him to pieces, like they did in all the movies.

Or maybe it was less complicated than that. Maybe the only guy who could save me was still just what he always was, still just a guy working in his basement and worrying that somebody else was going to steal the glory.

Trying to be as quiet as a weird clanky robot could be, I stood up and walked over to the door, pressing my fingertips to the frame and feeling for weakness. It was definitely something I could break through, so why wait?

Waiting around here was not going to be a good thing. I remembered again the vision of Captain Sellers and his guys ripping me to terrible pieces. I especially remembered the casual sneer on Sellers' face as he did it.

"Forget you," I said, giving the door a huge shove, and it ripped right off of its hinges, splintering into the hallway. *"Hooray,"* I said, feeling the soul of the monster rise in me again as I stamped out there and looked around.

SEARCH PARAMETERS screamed the flashing lights in my head. **EXIT STRATEGY . . .**

Forget exit strategy, I thought; *who cares about that?* Instead, I growled out loud, "How do I get out of here?" That produced an immediate reaction—muffled shouts and the running of feet. "Stop! Freeze!" voices yelled.

"You must be kidding," I said. I'd tried surrendering once before; it hadn't worked; so now I stepped down the hall and almost immediately felt the *thwack! thwack!* at the same time I heard gunshots.

92

"Don't let him get off the floor!" voices were yelling back and forth to each other. "Secure the stairs and elevators! We've got him pinned in!"

Secure the stairs and elevators, eh? Well, I thought, where I'm going, I don't need stairs or elevators. Bullets were bouncing off me as I stumbled down the hallway and straight through the glass window at its end.

I was in outer space now, flying, only . . .

Only I couldn't fly, of course. I was *falling*. In a second I slammed hard into the pavement below, instantly making a shallow hole.

It was dark. I thought at first I was knocked out, but when I heard more noises I realized I was just facedown in dirt.

Ouch . . . I think. That must have hurt, I mean, and it rattled the electronic senses a bit as I crawled up to stand and looked up to see where I'd fallen from.

The building stood above me, a threatening tower full of people who absolutely did not like me. I'd fallen seven stories, seven floors.

Leaving a big robot-shaped hole in the concrete.

Sirens were wailing, along with a loud klaxon bellowing, *ahoogah! Ahoogah!*

He who hesitates is lost—or, in this case, he who hesitates is recaptured by the Army and disassembled, so I got up slowly, it seemed. Rattling a bit more than before as I got moving, running for the fence line and freedom.

I ripped through chain-link fence as if it was . . . er, well, as if it was chain-link fence, but I was still strong enough to tear through. Then I took off on a flat run,

93

except at my robot pace it was more of a *clump-clump, clump-clump.*

They would be after me soon, I knew, and in force. There would be no fooling around this time, either. They would catch me and immediately switch me off to avoid more trouble. No pleasantly dramatic conversations with Mr. Robot Monster Boy, just a clamp on the back of the neck and then some cuts into the metal body to snip the appropriate wires, and then nothingness.

What happened when I got switched off? That would be a lot like dying, I figured. *An awful lot like dying . . .*

"This is Captain Sellers!" a voice was screaming now on a public address system. *"You're a smart little robot, but not too smart if you disappear into those woods. This is a restricted area and we've got mines planted all around the base. Do you want to get blown up? Do you?"*

Not quite, I thought, but that was okay because one of the neat little features in my computer brain turned out to be ELECTRONIC MINE DETECTION. I quickly scanned the field and my special visual system showed me exactly where the hidden obstacles were so I could tiptoe around them.

Arthur, I knew without any doubt, was not built to go into outer space. Who put mines in outer space? Arthur was a soldier robot.

So aside from avoiding exploding mines, how did I get out of here? *You're the soldier, Arthur; show me . . .*

Working with my robot senses, I tried concentrating on something my mind had told me earlier, my tracking and search equipment, which now clearly displayed:

94

RANGEFINDER TRACKING
XXP 10   XXP 20   XXP 30   XXP 40
ACCESS MINIMUM TARGET ACQUISITION CRITERIA
SORT TARGET—SELECT   !
—!—
!

INDICATED TARGETING (MARK xxxx)

So I was searching, but not for anybody. I was looking
for a way home. Except this wasn't going to be as easy—
easy?—as scrounging along before, because the Army
wasn't going to underestimate what some wacky robot
might do this time. They knew what to look for, and they
finally knew what to do once they caught me. I stared just
above the horizon at the stars and got myself an astronomi-
cal bearing to figure out where I was, how far from home
I was.

The system wasn't exactly precise. **ONE HUNDRED AND
TEN POINT SEVEN EIGHT MILES,** indicated my brain. But
it could have been off by a few yards . . .

Still quite a ways.

I moved on.

Walking through the woods at night again, I felt nervous
and anxious once more, just like I had in the beginning
of this adventure. The moon was full, but not as much as
it had been; clouds covered the light from time to time.

There are no coincidences in the universe, though, nothing that happens without reason. So as I trudged deeper
beyond the farmland, deeper into the woods, I came across
my old bearded buddy in the Army jacket, sitting in a

95

campsite near a pretty large clearing in the trees where the grass and bushes had been flattened down; it practically looked mowed. That was the only second I was actually startled enough that even my computer circuits jumped at the sight.

"Pssssst," I whispered.

He looked up as I revealed myself. "Hey, Walter," I said. "The lonely guy . . ."

"That's me," he said, looking up. "Oh, hello, Mr. Robot. It's okay, come on in."

"Max," I said, trudging over. "My name's Max, not Mr. Robot."

"That's right, Max."

"How are you, man?"

"I'm fine. Good, really. What about you? Need help? Still running from the Army?"

"Yeah," I admitted.

"Well, I'm glad they never caught you."

"They did. A couple of times."

"But you got away."

"I'm here now, but it doesn't look good."

"No?"

"No," I said.

"Well, who knows what might happen? It's a strange world."

"Tell me about it," I said. "So how did you get out here?" I asked.

"What do you mean?"

"Did you walk this far?"

"Not really. Me and Harry."

"Harry?"

96

"Yeah. You know Harry."

"No, I don't know any Harry."

"Sure you do."

I thought again but shrugged. "Sorry."

"You'll see. He'll be back in a minute."

"Okay," I said, starting to shrug again and ask another question, but there was no time, because then, without any warning at all and no chance to move, a helicopter roared down on top of us, blowing debris into the air, and I just stood there, knowing that this time it was all over . . .

12

CORY

"Not today, guys," I shouted at the helicopter, immediately making up my mind to fight. I stomped a step or two forward.

Here we go. My superhero moment. I was going to duke it out with the soldiers as they bounded from the chopper to grab me. If they wanted a war with a monster, then I was more than willing to give them one. *"Arrrrgggghhhh!"* I screamed.

Except Walter the lonely guy was up and running, too, and he wasn't running away, or toward the chopper; he ran to me. "Wait, hold it," he said, then turning back to the helicopter. "Easy, Harry, easy!"

Harry?

A new voice spoke then, crackling apparently from nowhere—from the helicopter. *"Hello, Max. How are you?"*

It took a second for me to realize the voice was the stealth helicopter, the one I'd talked with, the one who got a piece of my personality. He was talking out loud, through a slightly hushed loudspeaker, which made it sound as if the helicopter was whispering to us as its rotor blades shut down.

I was part computer, capable of processing almost anything, no matter how crazy (and how much crazier could anything be than getting your body stolen?), and even for me this was a bit too much to compute. "Harry? Your name is Harry?"

"Yes. I came across your friend Walter and knew him from my memory banks. He was alone down there and needed help, so since I knew he was a nice person and had helped you, I thought I'd help him. He gave me the name Harry."

"He named you Harry?"

"It's a nice enough name."

"I guess."

"That was scary," said Walter, telling his story. "This Army helicopter coming down after I helped you. But it's a weird world."

"A talking robot helicopter didn't surprise you?"

Walter shrugged, simply saying again, "It's a weird world."

"It's good to see you again, Max," said Harry the helicopter's mechanical voice aloud. *"I hope you are well."*

"Uh . . . I have my moments."

"The Army is still looking for you."

"How can you tell?"

"I'm an Army helo. I monitor military frequencies."

"But you're an escaped Army helicopter. So aren't they looking for you, too?"

"Yes, but I give off false position reports. And I have full stealth capabilities."

"So they can never find you?"

"Not never, but it would be very difficult for them."

That sounded good. "Man, I wish that was me," I said. "I wish this robot had stealth capabilities."

"Where do you want to go?"

"Huh?"

"Walter and I could take you."

"What?" I hadn't even thought about that.

"We're going to New York later, anyway. We could drop you somewhere."

Harry and Walter were going to New York? *Hmmm . . .* no time to think about that, though. Instead I said, "Yeah, I could use a ride. If you've got room."

"There's room," said Walter, as he started packing his stuff up and Harry the helicopter asked again, *"So where do you want to go, Max?"*

"Calpo," I said. "Take me back to Calpo . . ."

On the way, I decided I definitely needed help, so using the telephone inside my head, I called the only person I could trust. Cory was asleep—asleep?—and at first his mother wouldn't put him on the phone, but I told her it was an emergency. "Cory!" I heard her yelling. "The newspaper people are calling too early again!" (Cory delivered newspapers, something his mother never did appreciate.)

He finally came to the phone. "Yello?"

"Cory, man, it's me."

"Me? Okay, so who is 'me'?"

"Max."

100

There was a second of pause. "Max?"

"It's me, man."

"No way. This isn't Max."

Frustrated, I asked, "Why do you say that?"

"Well, first off, because you don't sound anything like Max."

"There's something wrong with my voice, man."

"Yeah? What?"

"That's a long story. I need your help, man. I'm in big, big trouble, but I've got an idea."

"Who is this?"

"Max. Can you get out for a while?"

"It's four in the morning, man. Are you crazy?"

What time was it? I didn't even feel tired. "So it's a little early," I said. "I'm your friend, remember?"

"Nobody's that good a friend."

"Come on, come on," I said. "You were getting up at five for the paper route anyway, right?"

"I dunno . . ."

"Cory . . ." I absolutely needed him to be sure it was me he was talking to, so I said, "Listen, Cory, I'm only saying this so you'll know it's me you're talking to. But you remember that thing you said to me about how you broke into your little brother's piggy bank to get money for those comics, and how—"

"Hey!" said Cory. "You said you'd never tell anyone that."

"I didn't, man. It's me, okay? The craziest thing ever is happening to me and I need your help. Will you sneak out?"

"I guess," he said. "Where are you calling from?"

101

"You'd never believe me even if I told you."

"Okay," he said. "I'll meet you at the streetlight. Give me a couple of minutes."

My plan was basically pretty simple. I was going to have Cory help sneak me up to the Abbotts' place and wait there for the crazy old guy to come and work out a way for me to get back my body. Maybe it was the last of the long shots, but it seemed the only thing left to do.

We were approaching Calpo, and Harry the stealth chopper came in at a lower altitude as he and I—and even Walter the lonely guy—kept a sharp lookout for my buddy Cory, who was bound to appear out on his street at any minute.

"Better set me down," I said to them. "It'll be bad enough for a robot to walk up and start talking to him. If I jump out of a helicopter, he might just fall over dead."

"Affirmative," said Harry, and they set down a few blocks away in a wide intersection and dropped me out. *"I'm on frequency 234-1180,"* Harry said. *"Call if you need help. Remember, I am heavily armed."*

"Thanks," I said, and they left me there to walk down and find my friend. The big whisper-quiet helicopter rose and disappeared just seconds before I saw Cory gliding by on his bike. I stepped out of the shadows and almost got him killed.

"Whoa!" yelled Cory, squeezing on his brakes and throwing his bike down, falling, and scrambling up in the same motion. I was two feet from his face and he wanted to get away fast. "No way!"

"Wait!"

"The robot guy!"

102

"Hold up, it's me, it's Max!"

"What?"

"It's me! Really! Wait up!"

This made him pause just long enough for me to hold his attention. I knew I looked like an alien from space in a football letter jacket, but that was okay for now. I said, "Cory, man, it's me, Max, and I'm in big, big trouble." I told him the short version of what had happened.

He looked like I'd just hit him over the head with a rubber brick; hurt, but shocked that it hadn't hurt more. "Stole your body? What are you talking about?"

"What do I look like I'm talking about? Look at me, Cory, I look like a spaceman, but it's me, Max, and those Abbotts are crazy mad scientists. But I need your help getting back up to see them."

"Why would you want to do that? If they did this to you, we are talking one major, major lawsuit . . ."

"I think it's too late for lawsuits, buddy," I said.

Cory stared at me a long moment before asking, "So how do you feel? Do you feel like a robot?"

"How is a robot supposed to feel? Who knows? I feel like something else besides me, that's for sure."

"What do you mean?"

I explained to him about the occasional machine flashes inside my head. "It's like exploding lightbulbs, but with words. Only sometimes there's not really words, it's just that the only way I could explain it would be to use words. It's strange."

"Yeah."

"You don't understand."

"No. But it still sounds cool. Like in a comic book."

103

"Exactly like in a comic book."

"You are one big tough-looking mutant," he said to me. "Do you feel strong, Max? Could you take on the world? Man, when I think about the things we could do . . ."

I had to tell my friend the truth. "I feel really kind of tired," I said. "It's like I'm inside a box, this robot box, and the whole thing is winding down around me. It's like I've got the remote control to the TV, but the batteries are dying so it only changes channels about half the time I click it."

"Man," Cory said in disgust, but that's all he said. He didn't ask what I thought about it, what I thought might actually be happening to me, and that was fine; who wanted to talk about that?

"Can you help me get to the Abbotts' place?"

"Sure," said Cory, his decision made. "I deliver their newspaper, don't I? Let's go find the old monster-makers . . ."

13

Desperate for Help

It was one thing to approach the Abbotts' little castle-house by parade of yellow schoolbuses in the daylight, it was another to creep up on it, wounded, in a manufactured metal body that was falling apart. In the dark. In the night.

Accompanied by a paperboy on a bike.

"Isn't the Army going to be looking around up here?" Cory was concered, looking up and around for helicopters and such. "I saw them a lot last night . . ."

"I don't think so," I said, hearing my voice sound somehow different, slower. "They won't know I got a ride, so they'll assume I'm walking around somewhere near the base."

"The base you escaped from."

"Yeah."

"Won't the Abbotts be looking around there, too?"

"I . . . I don't think so. I hope not. Abbott helped me get away, so he must know that I'll come here for help."

"Right . . ."

My voice definitely sounded different, and I definitely felt tired, so I made a check of my energy supply. There should have been nine hours or so left, but something was wrong—the energy in my batteries was draining faster than it should bave been.

A lot faster.

"Something's wrong," I told Cory. "I think the bullets and the water and the fall and all that have broken things inside of me. I . . . I don't feel so good."

"Hang in there, buddy."

"I . . . I'm trying . . ."

My robot body was starting to clink a lot more, and it was easy to see it was starting to fall apart. I decided to try and avoid talking as much as I could in order to conserve energy.

"Maybe you're solar powered," Cory suggested.

"Huh?"

"The sun'll be up anytime now. Maybe you're solar powered and that will help."

I didn't think I was solar powered, but I didn't want Cory to get scared, so I shrugged. "Maybe. Besides, even if the Abbotts can't . . . or won't . . . help me get my body back right away, they must have a way to fix my power problem."

"Maybe they could change your batteries, or something."

"I hope."

"So what are we going to do? Just knock on the door?" asked Cory.

"No," I said, shaking my head (something inside rattled—not a good thing). "I need you to do it. Mrs. Abbott might answer, and she hates me. She wants to have me taken apart."

"And old man Abbott likes you."

"I wouldn't exactly say 'like,' but he seems to feel guilty. I'm sure he'll help."

"The sun's up now, anyway. Feel any better?"

"No." If I'd been an animal, I'd have been howling in pain, and I almost did anyway, just to try and scare the Abbotts, who I knew must be hiding inside, worried about what their crazed creation might be up to.

Forget them, I thought. They deserved to share my pain, and if Mrs. Abbott was half as scared as I was, then terrific. Good for her. I—

Something jumped inside my head, flashed a bright, sudden light, and I realize now what it was: all these memories, all these events which have been taking place, the story I'd been telling. I've been trying to pace it out, tell it correctly and as it happened, but I'm running out of time.

It's like the beep of a dying cellular phone, or a camera battery. Time is running out fast, very fast, and there wasn't much time for detail.

We've arrived at the Abbott's place, and both the Abbotts and Cory are standing near me, but they won't believe me, and my power is slowly draining away.

Not was . . . *is* . . . not was . . . *is*. . . .

This is all happening *now* to me.

"You guys have got to help me," I say.

"No." Mrs. Abbott's one-word answer was cold, but I'm shocked because Abbott is crying—thick, heavy-looking tears rolling slowly down his scraggly face. It seems as if he wants so much to turn away from me, but he doesn't. Instead, he reaches out with his fingertips and actually touches the tip of my face; the *thunk* of his fingertips again reminds me of someone touching the Tin Man in *The Wizard of Oz*.

"You helped me escape," I say to Abbott, hearing now how my voice is dragging like a slow tape recorder. "You . . . you helped me . . ."

"I wanted to keep you from the Army's disassemblers, boy . . ."

"So help . . . me . . ."

"I will, lad . . . but I can't help you the way you want. Not the way you want . . ."

My mind—my brain, both brains now—are flashing and clicking.

I can feel the loneliness in Abbott's eyes, and it's him feeling it now.

Me and Abbott. His is the heart that is breaking.

"I need you . . . to help me," I say.

"You truly do not understand," Abbott tried to explain to me, fighting for control of his own emotions as he does, as I fade. "You're not who you think you are. You are the copy, thinking itself to be the original. The boy . . . Arthur . . . we can help you. We can help you understand what—who—you really are."

"I'm Max Helvey!" I tried to scream, but nothing much comes out.

It barely came out at all. "I'm Max Helvey," I say. "Don't you guys understand what you've done to me? What you're doing to me?"

108

Neither Abbott nor his wife are looking at me. But I could feel their gazes shooting through my insides. No, not their gazes; something else.

Their pity.

They didn't believe me at all. They think I'm some machine totally out of control. Some monster they created and are unable to convince, or help.

This is a waste of time and energy, and there's so little energy left inside of me. That much I know. STATUS: CRITICAL, said my internal readouts.

Wonderful.

So what am I supposed to do? Wreck the lab again and see how far I can get trying to track myself down? I tried that, and all that occurred was disaster.

I've never felt so tired and awake at the same time in my entire life.

Does this count as part of my life?

"This . . . this isn't ending the way it's supposed to," I say, feeling tired, so very tired. Way beyond what I've ever felt from playing baseball, or staying up late to watch New Years' Eve, or anything like that—my joints felt like they were stiffening up, as if in a few minutes . . .

I can't move my legs.

I can't move anything.

I am the Tin Man.

Frozen.

"Help me," I say. Just a whisper now, begging for the oilcan.

"There's nothing I can do," says the thing in my body. Max, my own face, looking down on me, as if I am the machine, as if I am the mistake . . .

109

Where did he come from? How did he get here?
Lights flashing in my head now:

WARNING.
SHUTDOWN IMMINENT.
POWER FAILURE.
BATTERY BACKUP FAILURE.

"I . . . " I start to speak, but there's no point; no noise is coming out anymore.

So I use what's left of the power supply to activate **RECORD, SAVE DATA.**

Somehow, maybe, I can save my thoughts, my memories of all of this, somehow save myself so that later—

INCORRECT CODE—PLEASE REPEAT PROCESS.

Except I—
Still no sound; everything is going black now, and—

SYSTEM SHUTDOWN.
SYSTEM TERMINATION—end messages.

14

THE END

So I stood there, looking and not believing what I was seeing. Max Helvey, idea guy, and I had no idea what to do or say.

Ever since they'd disconnected the screaming robot from me in the Abbotts' lab I'd been worried—when life turned into a comic book, like it did then, nothing was going to go down easy. When he'd broken out and shown up at the football game, I knew things were really exploding.

Now the explosion was over, but I still felt queasy and sick to my stomach. I stood beside my best friend Cory and we looked down at . . .

Me. I had to admit it was a little bit me.

At my feet was a robot that had completely believed it was me; its thoughts were what mine really would have been, had my brain been switched into the robot instead of copied. It was copied so perfectly, the robot thought it was the victim, the guy in trouble.

111

It felt alive, and it believed. It was continuing my life down another road, and then the batteries ran out.

"That's so cruel," I said.

"Yes," agreed the Abbotts. "How you must have . . . I mean, how he . . . *it* . . . must have suffered."

"We'll be able to know fairly precisely," said Mrs. Abbott.

"Say what?"

"What he went through. We'll be able to replay it, rewind the tapes. It's a computer chip, actually. We can replay it. Learn from them."

"What?" The whole concept seemed a little bit frightening to me, a bit shocking, and not just to me. Cory looked just as disgusted as I felt.

"The memory was stored, just like on any computer. He's just out of power now, shut down."

"So if he's repowered, he restarts from where he left off?"

"Oh, no," said Abbott. "The system would reboot. He'd start from scratch, from the first thought he had when he awoke and he thought—it thought—that it was you."

That seemed a horrible, terrible thing to even consider. "So he'd be as scared as he was the first time. He'd have to go through it all over again?"

"Well, yes, in a way, but we'd control the environment a bit better this time. We'd never let him break out of the lab. We'd use a restraint clamp to—"

I just stared at them.

I didn't say a word. I let the look on my face, and Cory's, tell it all.

It was Mr. Abbott himself who finally understood, and

112

stepped down to the still robot. Abbott brushed his red hair from his face, and bent over, pulling something from inside the robot's chest—a chip of a metal cartridge no larger than a microcassette tape. "Here," he said, offering it up.

"What's this?"

"This is you. The part of Arthur that was you."

My personality. My memories. My life, all reduced to something they might have copied and copied and sold like it was a CD in a music store, for people to like and use or not like and throw away.

That was scary.

Now my heart was pounding, and I accepted the heavy bit of metal into my hand. I stared at the thing.

"I'll play it when and if you decide you want to see it," Abbott said. "We owe ya that much, laddie. Think about it awhile."

"I will," I said.

Mrs. Abbott tried to make a joke of it, and it almost worked. "Hang onto that," she said. "It's an exact copy of your brain, and you never know when you might need a spare, do you?"

"Yeah, right," I said.

I was wondering what to do with my robot brain . . . wondering if there was any way to do something right for it. *What had he gone through?* I wondered. Me as a robot monster. *Who had he met? What had he learned?*

Who had he hurt?

And since the whole thing was a memory he'd written the way he'd wanted it, what had he lied about?

Was *Gimme Back My Brain* so terrifying it almost overloaded your system for good? Well, pull yourself together 'cause there might be a witch in the neighborhood— check out this unnerving preview of *YOUR TURN—TO SCREAM,* the new Avon Camelot Spinetingler coming in August 1997.

Michael stopped in front of the Creepy House and looked across the lawn. Kids still talked about this place. One of the windows was broken and a piece of cardboard was taped over it. Paint was peeling like long strings of paper from the porch railing. No one was outside. Not even the old woman who still scared little school kids with her wild eyes and her mop of silver white hair.

Michael stood, scanning the stuff on the lawn. There were sawhorses with sheets of plywood on top of them and old brown card tables, all loaded with the usual garage-sale junk. Nothing too interesting. There were can openers and eggbeaters and wooden spoons. Michael noticed a dead microwave with a crack down the door. There were sweaters piled on a table next to a stack of wooden salad bowls. Michael had two dollars in his pocket, but he couldn't see anything at all that he would want to buy. He was about to go on when he noticed a table on the other side of the lawn, stacked with boxes. Stuff that hadn't been put out yet?

Michael glanced back toward the old house. Where was she? It would be interesting after all this time to get a close look at the Creepy House Witch, maybe even talk to her a little. He would be able to tell Jeff and Don about it. They had cruised Foster Drive with him during the summer after second grade, hoping to catch a glimpse of the spooky old woman. Then they'd pedal their bikes away fast, giggling and scaring each other by making up stuff all the way home. Poor old lady. He hoped she had never noticed them, or if she had, that she had just thought they were silly kids playing some game.

Michael stood still a few more seconds, then made a sudden decision. He was in no hurry to get home and face Jeremy's questions. He turned off the sidewalk and crossed the lawn, glancing up at the house every few seconds. His heart was beating a little faster than it needed to and he almost laughed out loud. He was still a little scared of the Creepy House Witch, he admitted to himself, smiling.

"Can I help you?"

The voice, cracked and ragged, came from *behind* Michael. He turned back toward the sidewalk, his heart racing now. There she was. He swallowed and tried to talk sense into himself. She was a perfectly normal white-haired woman who just didn't have the time or the money

115

to keep her house up. That was all. To be afraid of her was absolutely idiotic.

"I asked if you needed help," the old woman said. "It would be polite of you to answer." She was frowning.

Michael shook his head, taking a step back to hide his nervousness. Her hair was cottony and wild and her eyes were odd somehow, but, he kept telling himself, she was not a witch. No one was a witch. She was looking at him very closely.

"I had been hoping you would come by one day," she began, then sighed, looking at him closely, her head tilted. Michael nodded as though he had understood and took one more step away.

"You like games, don't you? I seem to remember that you and your friends like games."

Michael had no idea what to say. Did she remember him? How could she? Lots of kids had gone past her house, scared and curious. He had never spoken to her. Not a single word.

"You do like games?" She sounded annoyed now, and she cleared her throat. "Well, look through the boxes up there." She gestured. "There's one I think you might like."

Michael glanced at the still-closed cartons he had noticed earlier. He backed up one more step, then turned and strode across the lawn. He would just take a quick look to be polite, then he would go. If there was something cheap he could buy, he would, just to make himself feel a little less guilty for riding past on his bike all those times, for peering up at her windows and acting like he was being chased as he pedalled off. He had never thought about what it must have been like for her to have so many kids curious about her.

Michael looked back at the old woman. She still looked angry. He walked a little faster, uncomfortably aware that she was watching him as he stopped and looked down into the boxes. They were empty. Puzzled, Michael looked up again, then back down into the boxes.

"It's there," the old woman called. "It's there." She pointed at the largest carton.

Michael looked again. This time he noticed a flat leather case lying at the bottom of the biggest box. He reached down and pulled it out. It was dusty and stained. "Is this what you wanted me to see?" he asked the old woman. She smiled, but did not react in any other way.

Michael turned the case in his hands. There was an old brass clasp. He undid it and tipped the case, holding it so that nothing could spill out. There was some kind of a playing board inside. It looked old. Michael hated board games. Jeremy usually cheated. Now that Michael was old enough to realize that, they rarely played.

Michael closed the clasp again and heard a jingle from inside the leather case. "I had better get going," he said politely. He set the case back in the box.

The old woman shook her head. "Not until you look at it." Michael shrugged, feeling uneasy. He stared at her. She was really small—not very tall and really thin. She reminded him of a scarecrow. "Open it up. Take a look. I am certain you are going to like it."

Michael shrugged again and lifted the leather case out of the box. There was something weird about the old woman, he decided, as he undid the clasp again. He would look at the game, but then he was going home. It wouldn't help anything to put off dealing with his brother anyway. Jeremy wouldn't be nicer in an hour. It wasn't like getting home late would make Jeremy forget to ask about the tryouts.

Michael tipped the leather case, sliding the game board out, careful not to drop any of the game pieces that were caught inside the case. He heard them jingle again, but he didn't bother to take any out. He set the case on the table and opened the board out flat, bending over it to look at it.

"Ever see anything like that?" the old woman asked.

Michael shook his head. He had been expecting an old checkers set or something. This was much more interesting. There were painted scenes on the board—and it really looked like paint, not like printed paper glued onto cardboard. He leaned over the board for a closer look.

"You won't see anything like it. Not ever again," the old woman said from behind him. She was so close that it startled him and he turned as she laughed a little, patting at her cottony hair. "I don't know if there's another one like it anywhere. I certainly have never seen one."

Michael looked back at the board. There were odd landscapes and swirling clouds. The path that a player had to follow ran through a lot of different scenes. The paintings had incredible detail in them. There was one of a forest—and he could see tiny painted spiders in webs. There were ornate circles and triangles. Michael wondered what they meant.

"How much do you want for this?" he asked, looking up.

The old woman had her hands on her hips. "You probably don't have enough. It's old and valuable."

Michael nodded, folding the board closed. "It looks like an antique. Where did it come from?"

The old woman bristled. "Do you really feel like that's

118

any of your business?'' She was frowning again, her old, familiar, unfriendly self.

Michael slid the board back into its case. ''Thanks for showing me. I better go home now.''

''Wait.'' It was a command. The old woman was staring at his face again, as though she was trying to remember something. Michael fidgeted, wondering if she really did recognize him. ''How much money do you have?''

Michael shook his head. ''Not much. Two dollars.''

She nodded briskly. ''Done. It's yours.''

Michael smiled, surprised. ''Are you sure?''

The old woman did not return his smile. ''Oh, yes. I was hoping you would come by sometime. I knew you liked games.''

''Well,'' Michael said, reaching into his pocket for the money, ''I appreciate this. I know it's probably worth a lot more than that.''

The old woman smiled. ''I want you to have it.''

Michael stepped closer, holding out the bills, crumpled from his jeans pocket. The old woman took them with a quick, snatching motion. He felt the dry, rough touch of her fingers for a split second. Then she was turning around, walking away from him. ''Go on, then. And share it with your brother.''

Michael nodded automatically and started walking, eager to get away from the old woman. He was back on the sidewalk and a few houses down the block before he realized what she had said. How did she know he had a brother? And why would she care who he shared the game with?

ABOUT THE AUTHOR

Novelist M.T. COFFIN, whose "Spinetinglers" novels have sold more than one million copies, began his career writing obituaries as a freelancer for his local newspaper, *The Nightly Caller*. This was in addition to his full-time job in the Dead Letter Department of the post office. While he thoroughly enjoyed writing about the dead, M.T. Coffin abandoned that work to begin his first novel when a series of nightmares so amused and delighted him that he felt he must write them down to share with his friends and family. He wrote thirteen "Spinetinglers" before his wife, Berry A. Coffin, convinced him that the stories were interesting and exciting enough to share with others and helped him to submit his manuscripts to Avon Books for possible publication. The books were accepted immediately and the "Spinetinglers" series was born when the first novel, *The Substitute Creature,* was published in March 1995.

Gwen Montgomery, of the Young Readers Department at Avon Books, is delighted to be publishing M.T. Coffin and says, "My spine tingled on the very first page and I knew right then that M.T. Coffin's books would keep readers dying for more."

M.T. Coffin was born on October 31 in Death Valley, California. The year is uncertain since, for some mysterious reason, all records of his birth except the date have disappeared, and no records of any family members have ever been discovered. Raised as an orphan, M.T. Coffin attended Death Valley High School. After graduation, he attended DeKay University where he studied literature. It was there that he was introduced to the works of authors who were to be among his lifelong favorites, including Bram Stoker, Mary Shelley, H.G. Wells, Jules Verne, Mark Twain, and Edgar Allan Poe. It was also there that he met Berry during a blood drive on campus. Berry received a Bachelor of Arts degree in elementary education from DeKay and today is a substitute teacher and bee keeper.

Now, M.T. Coffin is writing full-time and has just completed *Your Turn—to Scream.* Works in progress include *The Curse of the Cheerleaders, Wear and Scare,* and *Lizard People.* He is currently traveling to research upcoming novels and has most recently visited Transylvania in Romania and Murderers Creek, Oregon. Other "Spinetinglers" by M.T. Coffin include *Billy Baker's Dog Won't Stay Buried, My Teacher's a Bug, Where Have all the Parents Gone?, Check It Out—and Die!, Simon Says, "Croak!,"* and *Snow Day.*

M.T. Coffin lives in Tombstone, Arizona, with Berry and their two children, Phillip A. Coffin and Carrie A. Coffin, and their dog, Bones. He enjoys many hobbies, including reading, collecting books, taxidermy, playing the pipe organ, and bug collecting, an activity the entire family enjoys. The Coffins split their time between Arizona and their summer vacation home in Slaughter Beach, Delaware.

121

When asked about "Spinetinglers" and his many readers, M.T. Coffin responds, "I get goosebumps every time I think about how exciting it is to be able to tell stories all the time, and to reach so many people. I plan to keep writing forever."